P9-DIH-446

"*We Show What We Have Learned* introduces readers to the brilliant mind of Clare Beams. It has the hair-raising electricity similar to that of a new generation of writers that includes Karen Russell, Diane Cook, David James Poissant, and Kelly Link, yet reads with the stateliness of a bygone era."

—Shelf Awareness

"Stunning and brilliant. Clare Beams has a gift for illuminating one character's most private moment, causing the impact to transform the fates of many. She navigates the tightrope between inner and outer reality. The range of her stories is astonishing—funny and devastating, suspenseful and mesmerizing."

—Ursula Hegi, author of *Stones from the River*

"These amazingly inventive stories reveal an imagination rare in its command and courage. In gorgeous prose that thrills, instructs, and thoroughly inspires, Clare Beams obliterates the 'dividing line between possibilities and impossibilities,' showing how our passions can rule with reality-bending magic."

—Chang-rae Lee, author of *On Such a Full Sea*

"These stories are at once spooky and lush, eerie and deeply felt, ghostly but also vibrantly alive. Clare Beams is a magician, and each of these stories is a muscular, artful haunting."

—Caitlin Horrocks, author of *This Is Not Your City*

WE SHOW WHAT WE HAVE LEARNED

WE SHOW WHAT WE HAVE LEARNED

& OTHER STORIES

CLARE BEAMS

LOOKOUT BOOKS

University of North Carolina Wilmington

Second printing, April 2017
ISBN: 978-1-940596-14-3 | E-BOOK: 978-1-940596-15-0

Cover art © Andrea Wan
Cover lettering by Jane Molinary and interior design by Megan Ellis and Kate McMullen for The Publishing Laboratory

"On a Painting by Wang the Clerk" by Kenneth Rexroth from *Flower Wreath Hill*, copyright © 1979 by Kenneth Rexroth. Reprinted by permission of New Directions Publishing Corp.

LIBRARY OF CONGRESS CATALOGING-IN-PUBLICATION DATA
Names: Beams, Clare, author.
Title: We show what we have learned and other stories / Clare Beams.
Description: Wilmington : Lookout Books, University of North Carolina Wilmington, 2016.
Identifiers: LCCN 2016030212 (print) | LCCN 2016039710 (ebook) | ISBN 9781940596143 (pbk. with french flaps : alk. paper) | ISBN 9781940596150 (e-book)
Classification: LCC PS3602.E2455 A6 2016 (print) | LCC PS3602.E2455 (ebook) | DDC 813/.6–dc23

Lookout Books gratefully acknowledges support from the University of North Carolina Wilmington.

Printed by Thomson-Shore in Dexter, Michigan
17 18 19 TS 4 3 2

LOOKOUT BOOKS
Department of Creative Writing
University of North Carolina Wilmington
601 S. College Road
Wilmington, NC 28403
lookout.org

For my family
with my whole heart

Contents

HOURGLASS

"A TRANSFORMATIONAL EDUCATION," the newspaper ad had promised, so we went to the Gilchrist School to find out whether that promise could include me. With its damp-streaked stone and clinging pine trees, the school looked ideal for transformations, like a nineteenth-century inva-lids' home, a place where a person could go romantically, molderingly mad. I could almost sense my parents thinking that no one would find me here until I was done. For the first twenty minutes of my admissions interview, Mr. Pax, the headmaster, poured words upon our heads and seemed to require none from me. I had only to sit while he spoke of the crimes of modern education, the importance of avoid-ing the craze of the moment and what he called "the great, all-too-often-meaningless noise of exhibition," how he thought of teaching as a process of shaping, honing, turning each young woman into the best possible version of herself. My mother, who had never been anything but her own best version, smiled winsomely and told him, "We would just love to see Melody *blossom*, that's all."

This was the same word she'd used when she'd first brought the newspaper to show me in my bedroom, where I spent most of my time. "You might really blossom there, Melody," she'd said, laying the paper out gently on my quilt, and so I understood I couldn't stay at home anymore.

"Yes, yes," Mr. Pax told my mother now.

Next he inclined his great shining white-ringed head toward me. "Well, Melody! You've been quiet, for a person whose name heralds such mellifluousness! Please, tell me something about yourself. What activities do you most enjoy?"

A pause. Then, "Go on, Melly," my mother said, for all the world as if she expected me to rise to the occasion, except there was a little too much brightness in her voice. Had she really expected it, of course—had I ever shown any signs of such a capacity—we would not have been here. To encourage her in the encouragement, my father patted her back.

I dropped my eyes to the carpet and scoured my days for things I could speak of safely. School, which I hated. Television, which I knew better than to talk about here. Sleeping, which I liked, except when it ended. Drawing, a loose word for what I did sometimes, tattooing pages of computer paper in rhythmic, soothing swirls of ink. Reading Nancy Drew books, sticking and unsticking the pads of my fingers to their bright yellow, plasticky covers until I knew they were tapestried with whole invisible galaxies of my fingerprints. I never had anything to say about them when I was finished.

"Reading," I told Mr. Pax. The word came out scratchy and prematurely old-sounding. I hadn't talked much in the car.

"Superb!" He clapped, actually clapped, his hands. "And what are some of your favorite books?"

Somehow I had failed to foresee this question, though the floor-to-ceiling shelves on the wall behind Mr. Pax were lined and lined and lined with books like dull, uneven teeth. If I pretended to have read something impressive, Mr. Pax would certainly roll his chair over to the shelf and pull it out, set it right down on the desk between us for discussion. I could see myself sputtering and flecking the dusty damning rectangle of the book with spittle while my parents sagged.

"Mysteries," I said. "Mostly."

I waited for Mr. Pax's face to fall or flush with anger, for him to throw up his hands and cry, "This! This I cannot transform!" Instead he gave me a wide, warm illumination of a smile. "Ah, the pleasures of the whodunit," he said. "The neatness of the ending, a satisfaction that all too frequently evades us in life. You know what I've found to be true, Melody? A taste for mysteries is often the sign of a truly orderly mind."

My mind is truly orderly, I thought, cheeks reddening with hope and gratitude that dizzied me because I had been so unprepared for them. And next: *If this man wants to try to change me, I will let him.*

WE HAD DRIVEN TO GILCHRIST intending only to have a prospective-student visit, but after the interview my parents decided to leave me there that very afternoon, before I had a chance to lose something or fail to follow through on some simple instruction and force Mr. Pax to reconsider his assessment of me.

"You don't *have* to stay forever, of course. Let's just see how things work out," my mother told me at the school's front doors, where my father had already collected his umbrella. "We'll send your clothes and things straightaway," she said.

3

She leaned in to kiss me, leaving behind a crisp little cloud of her perfume. I wanted them to go—I wanted Gilchrist to begin on me—but there was something about the idea of my mother sorting through my clothes and boxing them up, my father driving to the post office with them in the trunk of his car, that made me feel as if I had died somewhere along the way without noticing. My throat began to close with tears. I told myself that the next time they saw me, I would be so polished I would hurt their eyes.

"I have *tons* of clothes she can borrow until her stuff gets here," said my new roommate, a lithe girl named Sally Briggs, in cheerful defiance of the fact that nothing she would own could possibly fit me.

"Well, thank you, Sally, that's very nice," my mother said. My father gripped my shoulder. I knew he tried to put things he couldn't say into that grip.

Then the door banged shut behind them and they were gone.

"It's amazing here," Sally said as she led me to the dormitory wing. "You'll see." She swung a door open into a small square of a room, kindly pretending not to notice that I was crying. "I'm super excited," she said. "I figured I'd get a roommate eventually. I was the only one with nobody. Odd number." I went in and sat on one of the desk chairs, trying to whisk my eyes dry with soggy fingertips. "Let's find you a dress for dinner," Sally said.

"That's okay," I said thickly.

Sally surveyed me. "We all wear dresses here, though."

"All the time?"

"Mr. Pax says how you look is the first impression you make on the world." She was in the closet now, pushing hangers aside with a brisk metal sound like the opening of a shower curtain. "And the easiest part to control."

I glanced down at my lumpish, besweatered form. My experience held no support for that idea.

"Here's the one I was looking for," Sally said.

The dress was black and had a forgiving enough stretch to contain me. I sweated through the fabric at the armpits almost immediately, but the color didn't show it. *Dresses*, I thought, as I pulled at the hem. *We all wear dresses here.*

THE HATS I LEARNED ABOUT a few days later, when I tried to take my copy of *The Mystery at Lilac Inn* outside during lunch. This was allowed: lunch and dinner were served on gray tin trays that you could take wherever you wanted to go, in the school building or on the three-acre grounds. At lunch you just had to be back at the tables by half-past twelve for Assembly. Routine was sacred at Gilchrist—the days were shaped to run in a smooth way that made your level of contentment mostly irrelevant—and so I felt unfairly accused when I looked up from the tricky balancing project of my tray and book and found Miss Caper in my path.

"Where are you off to? Outside?" she asked, tugging at the tie of the hat string beneath her chin, gazing at me from beneath the brim. Her rapid fumbling made her look even younger than usual, and always she looked young enough that the first time I'd seen her, standing before her blackboard full of notes on *Tess of the d'Urbervilles* on my first morning at Gilchrist, I thought she was a student.

"There's time still," I said. "Right?"

"Oh, yes. Just—it's bright out there. Why don't you borrow this?" She'd succeeded in working the knot free, and before I could respond she settled her hat on my head. It shaded my view of her. She was already moving off toward the faculty table, but I saw her stop and lean briefly over Sally, who looked in my direction and hurried toward me with a tube in her hand.

"Here," Sally said, squeezing something onto her fingers, and then she rubbed it—cold, cold—onto my face. Holding my tray the way I was, I couldn't use my hands to stop her. "Sunscreen," she said. "We wear it when we go out in the daytime. Hats too."

"Why?"

"The skin," Sally said, "should be like a beautiful blank page."

I sat under a tree. Nancy was about to figure out what was going on with the ghost, but I was having trouble paying attention. The paper of the book itself was distracting me, its even, frictionless feel beneath my skimming fingers. A caterpillar fell onto my lunch tray, into my salad dressing. I watched it writhe.

At 12:25 I closed the book and carried everything back in to rejoin the thirteen other girls in my year. I took off the hat and pinned it under my arm as I approached the table, careful not to crush it, wondering where I could put it so no one would notice it and understand that Miss Caper had needed to loan it to me. I banged my knees as I took my seat, and the girls all turned in my direction, no particular expression on their faces, before settling again into elegant disinterest. I sat there feeling, as always in such moments, my mother's eyes. The hat I tucked into my lap like a house pet that had proved embarrassing.

Mr. Pax rose. Every day he made a speech to start Assembly. I listened as closely as I could to each of them, filing away as much as possible in the hope that it would teach me how to become what everyone was trying to make me. Even without effort I would have remembered entire sentences—he had that kind of voice, those kinds of words. *To unlearn an old habit takes more diligence than to learn a new one,* he'd said to us the day before. The day before that: *Remember that the true intellect requires so much energy to sustain that it has none left over to devote to display.* His own speeches, we understood, were not the same as the display of which he spoke. Though Mr. Pax strutted daily before us, shone, dripped words like syrup, everyone knew that this was not artifice. The artifice would have been to prevent himself from doing these things.

At the front of the room, Mr. Pax began to speak. "Today, girls, I thought I might share with you a brief history of Assembly itself."

He waited while small conversations quieted. Sally swiveled toward him in her seat.

"When I came to Gilchrist, more years ago than I would care to disclose,"—the faculty, lined behind him at their table, tittered softly—"I came armed with the belief that education is nothing less than the shaping of the soul. Thus, upon my arrival, I had to ask myself: these souls entrusted to me, what form ought they to assume? What shape would best suit them? It was a question neither asked nor answered lightly, but eventually, an answer did come. I realized that I wished to mold not future citizens of the world as it was, but of the world as it should be. For it is my belief that the world around us has lost the grace and purity it had in earlier times, girls. That does not, however, mean that *you* need do so. It was—is—my deepest wish to prepare you to stand in loveliness before eyes that no longer see as they ought, to answer with eloquence the questions of those who may or may not be capable of appreciating what they hear. I believe this sort of deportment has value no matter how it is perceived. At the end of the day the world is not my concern. *You* are."

The skin on my arms prickled. I ran my fingertips over the bumps, trying to settle them into blankness.

"In light of all of this, I consider Assembly a sort of training ground, if you will, for your lives to come. When you stand and make announcements—even if you are simply questing after lost items or marking the anniversaries of one another's birth—you are practicing being seen and being heard. And it is my most cherished hope that you are also considering, deeply, how you wish to appear and to sound in those moments."

I scanned the two lines of girls at my table, the willowy forms and the smooth smooth faces, behind each of which was a fluid voice at the ready. I knew just how I wished to appear and to sound. Very soon I would understand how it was done.

ON A CRISP THURSDAY near the beginning of November, Miss Caper stood in a patch of sun at the front of the classroom and talked to us about Keats and negative capability. We watched her from our circle of desks, the same desks as at my old school, with chairs barred to the tabletops to prevent the tiltings-back of unruly boys. Not a one of us, of course, would have been inclined to tip; we were to remain, generally, as still as possible. "Let your minds be nimble from within a state of comely repose," Mr. Pax told us.

Miss Caper wrote "'Ode on a Grecian Urn,' 1819" on the board, rounding the letters prettily. Then she put down the chalk and began to read to us in a low, thrilled voice: "Thou still unravished bride of quietness, / Thou foster-child of silence and slow time..."

She read the whole thing, though we had also read it for homework, while we clicked our pens or wrote the title and date we already knew in our notebooks. When she finished she looked up and breathed deeply. "He was *twenty-three* when he wrote that," she said. I had been thinking for a couple of days now that Miss Caper might be a little in love with Keats.

She asked us what we thought the poem meant. I'd read it swimmily, floating in its currents, and had come away with the vague sense that it was saying something about art. I kept this sense to myself. I never volunteered at these times, since the potential cost of a wrong answer mattered much more to me than the potential benefits of a right one. The other girls were not cruel—we were kept too busy for cruelty—but

I didn't trust them. For the most part they ignored me, even Sally, who often seemed oblivious of my presence, in a friendly way, while we were actually speaking. I had not become the way they were. I tied my hair back into the right modest knot, and I wore the right things, the hats and the sunscreen, the dark dresses, black, burgundy, brown, gray. But my skin had stayed freckled instead of going paper-blank. No new voice had blossomed in my throat. And the dresses did nothing to make me look like the others, who filled their own with foreign undulating shapes.

Near the end of class, Miss Caper called on Lila, who was talking about the *imagery* of the poem, which she really thought was just so *powerful*, when the bell rang. Lila stopped talking instantly. "'Eve of St. Agnes' for tomorrow!" Miss Caper told us, as we closed our books and began to file away from her. "Answer the questions at the end of the poem, please."

"Melody," she said then, shocking me into stillness, "a moment?"

She leaned against the edge of her desk. I walked back toward her and stopped, leaving a safe berth between us.

"Have a seat," she said, pulling one of the desks out of its circle, closer. I sat. "I've been asked to speak to you." She paused, leaned in. "You've been here over a month now."

Words rose within me, tasting of panic, pleas for more time and promises of improvement—but I knew that if I tried to release them they would only clog in my mouth. I waited. Miss Caper's eyes flicked back and forth between mine, as if the right and left were delivering different messages to her.

"We think you're fitting in nicely. Really we do. You do re-member what Mr. Pax says about the outside and the inside, though?"

I tried to call up the words, which I recognized from one of his recent speeches. Miss Caper gave me only a few seconds before filling in the answer herself. "He says that the outside should as nearly as possible match the quality of what's within. That way, we do everything in our power to give those whom we encounter the right expectations. So a lovely person, like you, should do her best to look lovely."

She paused again. "Melody," she said, her voice thrumming the way it had when she'd recited the Keats poem, "how would you like to *look* a little more like a Gilchrist girl?"

She walked over and opened a closet I had never noticed in the corner of the room. From within it, she produced a hollow stiff shell, trailing long tentacular laces.

"A corset," she said.

There was a flourish in her wrists as she held it out to me. A new form, right in her hands, ready for the taking.

AFTERWARD, I SWISHED my way up the stairs, pausing every two to breathe, and into our room.

Sally had been reading on her bed. "Oh, thank God," she said when she saw me. "I was getting so sick of having to get dressed in the bathroom. I don't know why they didn't just let me tell you. Miss Caper laced you up?"

I nodded. Miss Caper had, after turning away discreetly while I pressed the front of the thing to myself. The pulling of the stays had hurt. I had not made any sound, though. I told myself I was having every faulty disappointing breath I had ever breathed squeezed out of me.

"Let me see." Sally stood and slid a hand down the back of my dress. She tested the stays with a practiced finger. "Not very tight," she said. "I'll do it better tomorrow. We can lace each other now. All year I've been having to knock on Eva and Kate's door and get one of them to do mine."

I felt, all the rest of that evening, as if I were moving within a body that I had strapped on. The lacing seemed to be pulling me together in entirely new ways. I didn't want to take the corset off at bedtime, but Sally said I should, so I

undid it and draped it carefully over the back of my desk
chair before I climbed into bed. From my pillow I could see
the bright shape of it hovering in the dark.

The next day at Assembly, as I ate with my back straight
under the force of the lacing, Mr. Pax stood and said, "Miss
Caper tells me that the ninth grade has just completed its
study of Keats's 'Ode on a Grecian Urn.' A wonderful and
wise poem: 'Beauty is truth, truth beauty...' " He let his voice
linger. "One of the truest, most beautiful lines ever written,
perhaps. For our surroundings are so often ugly, girls. Why
should we not strive for beauty and bettering where they are
within our reach?"

His eyes brushed lovingly over us then. I could have sworn
that they paused for a special instant on me.

THE CORSET DID CHANGE the way I moved through my life.
My torso had become a stiff column, suddenly unbendable,
and I had to swivel my hips when I walked to compensate.
I couldn't quite breathe in fully, either. But it's surprising
how rarely a person needs to breathe to the very bottom of
her lungs in a day. Everything they asked of us at Gilchrist—
the essay writing, the graphing of functions, the discussing
of literature, the announcing of one another's achievements
at Assembly—could be accomplished while taking no more
than refined sips of air. It was only when somebody worked
herself up that there was trouble: the time Eva had a tantrum
over her essay grade in English, for instance, and went very
red and then slumped to the floor. Miss Caper produced
smelling salts from her desk drawer and stroked Eva's forehead while she came around. I watched from my own desk
and breathed evenly through the whole episode.

There was some pain: a compressed feeling and a peri-
odic but deep ache in the ribs. I took satisfaction in this.
It seemed to me proof of payment. Quickly I came to feel,

when I took my corset off to sleep at night, a disbelief that I had once walked around in that state, so unsharpened and unsupported, so greedy in my consumption of air and space. I would read my mysteries by flashlight beneath the tent of my sheets, after lights-out, and try to breathe shallowly still, so as not to stretch myself back out, as I followed Nancy's exploits. Nancy would never have needed a corset, would simply have willed herself into the proper contours, so that all her plots could unfold as a series of perfect pictures.

Our lacing-up in the mornings became a companionable thing between Sally and me. She was determined, much more determined than Miss Caper had been, hampered as she was by gentleness. One morning, after a couple of weeks had gone by, Sally finished pulling at me and then tugged me over, back first, to the full-length mirror on the inside of our door. "Look," she said. I peeked over my shoulder. "See that bump in the laces there? That's as tight as I used to be able to get them." I did see it, the kind of crimp that marks where the lace of an often-worn shoe hits the grommet— easily an inch below where the knot was now. Visible proof of what was being accomplished.

I turned back to her. "Tighter," I said.

"Tighter? Mel, it's already—"

"I want it tighter," I said. While she pulled, I closed my eyes to imagine the moment in which my mother would first see me. Her eyes widening at my new swell-dip-swell, her smile knocked out of carefulness.

Other changes came as my shape shifted. The rest of the girls were still not exactly my friends, but I could feel the distinction between us blurring. Sometimes they would call me over in the dining room even if Sally wasn't with me. I wrote letters to my parents (we were big on old-fashioned letter writing at Gilchrist) in a chatty voice I honed with pride. "Math will never be my forte," I told them, "but we all have our limitations! Hope you enjoyed the weekend with the Bermans!" In classes, I now spoke occasionally. I had realized the teachers were so generous that they would mostly spin a wrong answer right for you. Miss Caper seemed to have taken a particular shine to my reading voice. She called on me more than anyone else in the rotation; I read the Brownings, Tennyson:

> A curse is on her if she stay
> > To look down to Camelot.
> She knows not what the curse may be,
> And so she weaveth steadily,
> And little other care hath she,
> > The Lady of Shalott...

"The Lady of Shalott's death," Miss Caper said, "is *inescapable* once she sees Lancelot, rises from her loom, and looks to Camelot. Why is this, do you think?" she asked me. "What is the *nature* of the curse?"

"I guess..., " I said, "it's like she's supposed to be separate? Because of the weaving. So when she leaves she wrecks it?"

"Good," Miss Caper said.

She called on Melissa Clearwater to read "The Kraken." I let my hands drift for a moment to my waist, my habitual test, the patting-down of my dimensions. They were changed, they were definitely changed, and sometimes this brought me comfort. Other times, the curve in at my waist would feel too gradual beneath my palms, and I would press myself tight in fear. I was not yet changed enough. I would have to do better.

The harder I tried to resist these tests, I found—the more I tried to reassure myself that they weren't necessary, that of course my waist was becoming smaller and smaller as the days passed—the greater was my need for them.

One afternoon a few months into my wearing of the corset, Mr. Pax almost ran into me in the hall. He had his head down, bulleting forth to something important. I sidestepped him at the last instant and wobbled, my balance threatened. He looked up in surprise, then smiled. "Excellent save!" he said, reaching out to steady my slipping books. "My apologies!" He leaned back to look at me more closely. His eyes slipped from my face, down. "I must say, Melody," he told me, "that I hear wonderful things about you. I am very pleased."

He moved off down the hall and left me filled with such raucous joy that my heart rocketed and dappled my vision in shimmery patches, and I had to take very deliberate, measured breaths to steady it.

THREE WEEKS BEFORE the beginning of spring recess, our poetry readings took a sudden turn. Miss Caper arrived bearing two stacks of brand new, slim volumes, which she passed around the room.

"Page thirty, please," she said. "This poem is by Su Tung P'o. It is called 'On a Painting by Wang the Clerk of Yen Ling.'"

She began to read:

> The slender bamboo is like a hermit.
> The simple flower is like a maiden.
> The sparrow tilts on the branch.
> A gust of rain sprinkles the flowers.

Her voice was hesitant on the new, spare rhythms.

When she'd finished, we stayed quiet for a minute, trying to decide what to make of what had just happened. Finally, Sally raised her hand. "How is that a real *poem*, though?" she said. "Where's all the *description*? And the *rhyme* and everything?"

Miss Caper sighed. "There is a very deep, modest kind of beauty in the poem I have just read, girls. A beauty that stems from rendering a thing precisely and quietly in words." It sounded all right, but she looked somehow off-balance with such a small book in her hands. "This poem is made of a series of perfectly captured moments. I think you will come to understand, as we continue to read. You'll be working with pages thirty-two through thirty-eight of the anthology for your assignment this evening."

I stared down at the book before me. I lifted it. Its lightness made me anxious.

"But I thought we were reading 'Aurora Leigh' next," Eva said.

"As did I," Miss Caper told us. "The headmaster wishes to make a change."

"Why?"

"He is ever finding new forms of beauty to bring to our attention. Or, in this case, not new. Very old," Miss Caper said.

"Remember when he had us try taking milk baths, like Cleopatra? Until we started to smell," said Sally.

We laughed. The laughing relieved our nervousness a little. Even Miss Caper smiled, though her eyes glistened oddly.

Around this time, one of the sixth-graders—Lizzie Lewis, a pixie of a girl with a great mass of black shining hair—stopped showing up for meals, even Assembly. The sixth grade at large reported that Lizzie no longer came to classes either. Our curious whispers gathered momentum as the days passed until finally Miss Ellison, the math teacher, had no choice but to address them, if she wanted us to focus on the quadratic equations she had written on the board. "Lizzie is receiving special lessons from Mr. Pax," she told us, "for which she requires focused time alone." We could tell from the falsely confident way she said this that Miss Ellison didn't know what was happening either. Still, Lizzie's continued absence gradually became old news; we stopped talking about it because there was nothing new to add, and then we mostly forgot her.

I spent spring recess at Gilchrist, where I had also spent

Christmas vacation. My parents seemed always to be traveling during the times when I could have come home: Bora Bora, an Alaskan cruise. My guess was that my mother was unwilling to trade the newly poised girl she glimpsed through my letters for a flesh-and-blood me who might disappoint her in familiar ways, and my father was unwilling to challenge her. Time seemed to soften and stretch long in those two weeks. I missed Sally and her lacing. I couldn't get Kate, the only other girl from our year who had stayed at school for the break, to pull as hard. I knew for a fact that the ground I had gained was receding, because I could reach back and feel from the lacing how I'd eased back into ruts I thought I'd abandoned for good a week, two weeks earlier. When I touched this proof, this record of my spill back over the lines that had been drawn, powerlessness made me bite my tongue until I tasted metal. At night, I held my Nancy Drew books and ruffled their pages, the furred soft sound of the paper like another person's breathing in the empty room, but even this didn't help me sleep.

I would feel better once the others were back, I told myself. And anyway I *had* changed. I knew it. Yet it seemed to me, there in the dark, that any progress that could be undone in this way was not real progress at all. A nightmare vision of the first day of summer vacation haunted me, being driven home in my parents' car, its smell of leather and bits of food I had dropped over the years as familiar to me as the smell of my own body. I would see in my parents' faces, each time they snuck looks at me from the front seat, the brief flight and then the dead plunge of hope—teaching me over and over that I would always be the same as I had ever been.

ON OUR SECOND DAY BACK in session after spring recess, Mr. Pax stood up at Assembly and said, "I am sure you have all noticed that Lizzie Lewis has been gone from your midst for some time."

None of us had thought about Lizzie in weeks, but we nodded solemnly.

"Lizzie has undertaken a special project for me," Mr. Pax told us.

The concept of this *special project* brought a pang. I wondered what had distinguished Lizzie, made him choose her—in what particular ways I had failed.

"The project," Mr. Pax said, "has regrettably required her temporary absence from your company. But she is, at last, ready to rejoin you, and ready to show you the fruits of our labor. And what fruits they are, girls! Or will be, when they have ripened fully."

He paused and smiled at us. "You see, Lizzie is on her way to attaining a very ancient form of grace. One that will soon be made available to the rest of you, though it will be a bit more complicated for those who are older and have already grown more. Her initial break has been made, but of course that's really only the beginning. The binding process itself will require some time before we achieve the desired result."

We quieted and took in a breath deep enough to strain our laces.

Miss Caper stared at Mr. Pax. Her face was rigid. Mr. Pax's eyes found hers and held them as if this were a matter of will, though he was still smiling. Finally Miss Caper looked away.

"Recovery is still in the early stages," Mr. Pax said. "There are no shortcuts in such a process, girls. Walking remains for the future. So you'll pardon our rolling entrance. Lizzie, my brave butterfly!"

My eyes flew, with everyone else's, to where he pointed. But in the pause before Lizzie appeared, I saw others come one by one through the empty doorway, others I knew I was the only one to see. Without hurrying, each took to her place in the line. I knew them all instantly. The Lady of Shalott, bent from her loom yet graceful, one of her ivory arms banded in bright thread. The simple-flower maiden, petal-cheeked, lilting as if in a breeze. Nancy with her blond, metal-gleaming hair and the pressed slacks that fit her like her rightful skin. And my mother, my ever-lovely mother. My mother with perfection itself in her face. They all turned back to watch the door.

Then, in a wheelchair pushed by Miss Ellison, came Lizzie. She bore her abbreviated feet before her, propped on the rests: tiny hooves in child-sized slippers of a vivid blue silk.

It was a slow entrance, a grand one. There was pride in Lizzie's smile. Also pain, but that was the price, as all of us at Gilchrist had already learned. And if her pain was greater than anything we had yet experienced, what she had bought with that pain was proportionately greater too, I thought: a change that was not reversible. Lizzie would never have to sit in her room and tilt her folded feet this way, that way, wondering if a slow slide had begun that would carry them back to their previous dimensions. Here at last was certainty. Lizzie would feel the proof of her new and more beautiful self with each step she took after this, each hair's breadth of a footprint she left behind her, the way all that had anchored her to ordinariness had been whittled down to a fine, sharp point.

I caught sight of Miss Caper's face again. It had gone very white; her eyes were wide. She saw only the pain, I thought, and not that the pain was *for* something. I wanted to explain to her that after this, nothing could hurt Lizzie, not in any important way.

My mother and the others who had preceded Lizzie into the room were still arrayed in their line. They watched me approvingly. I turned to look at Mr. Pax, our great shaper, whose face was red with triumph. I thought that I was ready to feel my bones break between his hands.

SALLY DIDN'T SEEM TO WANT to talk and talk about Lizzie and Mr. Pax the way I did.

"I'm excited, of course," she said, opening her book and dropping her face down into it. "I'm just going to need a little time."

"For what?" I said. This idea of time, taking time, frightened me. I wanted all of us to jump together, right away. I could feel something gathering behind us—if we weren't quick it might catch us, stop us from leaping.

"Just for it all to sink in."

"What do you mean?"

Sally turned a page.

I told her I felt like a walk, though what I felt like was getting away from her and her new wariness. Down the hall my feet plodded. Struck the ground, slablike. How would they sound without all their meat?

Ahead of me, at the end of the hall, Miss Caper came out of her room. She pulled a rolling suitcase, a clumsy appendage that took the turn too wide, knocked against the frame of her door, and capsized. She muttered and turned to right it and so she saw me.

I thought about Lizzie and her spectacular entrance. Nobody would have seen Miss Caper's exit if not for me.

Miss Caper straightened her shoulders. "Hello, Melody."

"Where are you going?"

She waved one hand, but the other stayed tight on her suitcase handle. "Away, for a little while."

"He wouldn't bind *your* feet," I told her, "if that's what you're afraid of. You must be too old."

"That's not it." She released the handle now to clutch herself, cupping her elbows in her palms. "I just can't watch. I don't think I can watch."

Lizzie had managed to watch, and it was her own feet she was watching. Lizzie, maybe a year past giving her Barbies haircuts and drawing pictures of horses.

I raised my eyebrows, cruelly, politely, at Miss Caper. The expression felt familiar on my face, I realized with a wave of elation, because it belonged to my mother.

Miss Caper's mouth twisted. It trembled. But her fingers were steady as they began unbuttoning her dress. They worked until they'd made a large enough opening for her to slip her arms out and let the cloth fall away. Then she reached back and undid her stays. She tipped her corset to the floor.

Miss Caper, on whom I had never seen even an inch of skin above the wrists, stood naked from the waist up, there in the hallway. The corset had striped red slat marks into her skin. Her breasts hung large and pale, her hips shelved out, but her waist pinched neatly, as if large fingers held it so, just so. As if she wore the corset still. As if she *were* a corset, nothing but the filling-in of a corset, something poured inside to allow a corset to stand up, walk around, and go about its life.

"You see this, Melody," she said.

I nodded, though an answer didn't seem required.

"Mr. Pax has all the most wonderful plans, and the most wonderful reasons, he always has. But I don't know whose body this is." She held her hands out to me, displaying the garment of herself. "I hope," she said, "you never know what that feels like."

"But why would I want my body?" I asked.

She looked so sad then. I wished there were a Keats poem for the occasion I could recite, to show her that I saw what she'd tried to do, and that I was grateful. Maybe there was. I hadn't read that much Keats.

Miss Caper turned away and began putting herself to rights. She lifted the corset, pressed it to her front again. Then she hesitated.

"Could you?" she said softly, offering her back to me. The rows of laces like the ticks on a ruler, like the tines on a comb.

"Of course I could," I told her. I moved nearer. The corset gapped the way the lip of a wound does. I took the ties in my hands.

"Did you know I would be so good at it?" I said.

Her shoulders jerked, as if in response to a sudden noise.

I laced her up.

WORLD'S END

By the time the world's end job came to him, the architect was twenty-six but no longer considered himself young, if he ever had. He felt his professional life had begun. He shaped land, not buildings: he was a builder of landscapes, one of the first of his kind in New York, though this was the 1880s and Olmsted had already carved out Central Park, strange hole in time and space, in the middle of the skyward-straining city.

These were the days when wealthy people were just coming to realize what their commerce had paved and grimed over, and to miss that green in the pure religious way they missed the childhood of their earliest memories. The architect had a knack for making the lost thing feel less lost, for sculpting

expansiveness into a city courtyard. The clients who had
hired him for his five paying jobs so far seemed to consider
this a kind of magic. To the architect himself, summoning
space felt as simple as instinct. In the two-room apartment
on the Lower East Side where he had grown up with six
brothers and sisters, he had learned to thirst for it.

Still, even the architect could see that the World's End job
was one he had no real business having. It was no city courtyard. Robert Cale, the Boston businessman who owned the
land, hinted in his letter at vastness. Cale had heard about
the architect through a former trading partner, for whom
the architect had designed a plot the year before: vines
rioting over terraced rock, creating an effect like a shallow
green bowl. But Cale seemed not to know that the architect
had never had a job of this size and in fact had never even
been out of New York. "B. says you're the best," the letter
read. "Come convince me."

So the architect took a train to Boston. He tried to relax
into the motion of the car, as the prosperous-looking people
around him were doing. He did not like tight spaces, though,
had not since the week, in his thirteenth year, when three of
his siblings had died of the measles in his family's cramped
apartment. Finally, pinned against the window by his seat-
mate's arm, he managed the shallow hemmed-in sleep he
remembered from childhood, in which any kick or roll
brought contact with flesh.

When the train arrived, a carriage was waiting to take him
to Cale's. The drive took hours, and for all that time the architect couldn't stop staring out the windows. He was study-
ing the way money looked up here. The way it showed itself
in the stately, expressionless faces of the houses he passed.
He had long dreamed he might one day move freely through
houses like these, yet he had the feeling now that they were
judging him, as he went by, and finding him lacking.

The Cale house was no different, formidable atop its wide

green lawn. It had clearly been built by men who had forgotten how to build anything but ships: its whole bulk seemed to yearn forward, and a flagpole jutted from its wide white forehead at the exact angle of a bowsprit. Perhaps those long-ago builders had known water, the architect thought, but they had not understood land. They had flattened most of it and piled the rest beneath the structure, in a stylized bulbous hill that worried at his eyes. The effect was like a cherub's cheek carved into a living face.

The door of the house opened and a man the architect assumed was Cale walked out onto the front steps to survey the approaching carriage. The architect shifted nervously in his seat. Bennett, his former client, had told him that Cale had tripled his family's whaling fortune in the manufacturing of hosiery, then left the business. Something about this progression, open seas to delicate fabrics to nothing, had given the architect a vivid picture of Cale's features: a hawk's cutting beak swathed in trembly old-man wattles. But Cale in the flesh was broad chested, his hair still as black as the architect's own. When the carriage stopped and the architect climbed out, feeling travel-stained and stiff in the hips and knees, Cale offered a strong, perfectly smooth hand for him to shake.

"We walk from here," Cale said next. With no further greeting, let alone any offer of rest or food or drink, he started down the drive, crunching the gravel underfoot. The architect ran a few paces so he could walk alongside and not behind the man.

They turned left down the road. "The land's a peninsula," Cale told him. "I've bought it all up. Every farmer around here owned his piece, but nobody took much convincing. I know them—go out in the mornings sometimes and look my acreage over, same as they do—so they trust me. And they all decided their cows could eat grass somewhere else once they saw my offer." Cale laughed a big showpiece of a laugh. He spoke in hard bursts and had a bandy-legged way of walking, pivoting his shoulders from side to side as if he were trying to take on the elements. His vowels, though, had been pinched flat by fancy schools. "What I want to do is put up houses. Sell them. People said I should talk to somebody before I bring in the builders, to make sure we put everything in the right place." Then, with no audible pause, "You're younger than I thought."

"Well," the architect said, but couldn't think what to add.

"Course I barely had to shave when I opened my first factory."

After some steps in silence—they were coming to the end of the road now, the architect could see it up ahead of them, thick with trees—the architect asked, "How much land is it? Your letter didn't say."

"Just over two hundred acres, " Cale said.

The architect bit the insides of his lips with wanting.

"There are men I could hire in Boston," Cale continued. "But Bennett says you're different. Says he's never seen anything like the work you did for him."

The architect kept his eyes straight ahead, fearing the size of the plot he had designed for Bennett—fifty by seventy-five feet—would show in his face.

They traipsed through a small wood and then out into a waist-high meadow. It was October, but the sun had strength still. The air around them was warm with the fragrance of grasses and leaves, tinged beneath with the darker, richer breath of the coming decay and the tang of the sea, both of which could be tasted more than smelled. "From the top here you can see the whole of it," Cale said. They mounted a long hill, stripping off their coats. Halfway up they startled a covey of blackbirds from their hiding place in the grass. The birds chattered angrily and rose with much flapping, the red patches on their wings flickering like the blinking of eyes.

Then at last they were at the summit, and World's End was spread before the architect for the first time.

He had never before seen so much empty land beside the ocean. The greens and golds of it against the striated blues of the water were disorienting to him, beautiful in a way he had no means of storing within himself. The land lay in two bowed masses, separated by a thin strait, as if a round-headed long-necked creature had surfaced from the deep, and the architect and Cale stood on its curved back. At the coast was rock or cliff, and in the middle was pasture that had been sloppily cleared—a few big trees, too much trouble to cut and cart away, had been left standing—but he fell in love at once with the land's shape. It rolled and pitched as if it lived, as if it had only momentarily consented to be still.

Sheep speckled the hills here and there, grazing or wandering, made desultory by the sheer quantity of the grass that surrounded them. In the distance, across the water, the buildings of Boston could be seen. From World's End the city seemed jumbled, improperly put away. The architect looked and looked. Part of his mind was sculpting and planting and laying roads, while another part considered how he might go about seeming equal to this job, so that he might have it.

"Well?" Cale asked.

The architect saw that Cale had been watching him while he took in the land. It was too late now to hide his eagerness.

"When it's done, the whole world will want to live here," the architect said. He hoped his own face was alight with belief, or vision, or whatever it was that Bennett had promised he had. "I can start right away."

He'd meant to sound commanding, but he could hear the thinness of his voice. For a moment, he was sure that Cale would walk him back down the hill, close him into the carriage, and signal to the driver to take him away, that he would have to wonder ever after if World's End had been real.

Instead Cale smiled. "Right away sounds soon enough."

THE ARCHITECT SPENT THAT NIGHT in Cale's house, in a grim four-poster bed that made him feel laid out for a funeral rite. The next day he spent surveying World's End, learning its contours with his feet and eyes. He fingered leaves, and took notes, and made sketches, and dug his hands into the soil. Already he could not look at the land without seeing what he would do to it. He sought out the nooks where the houses would nest, out of one another's sight and where each would have its piece of the beauty that would be unlike any other. People liked to feel that they had the best of something. Roads striped the green in the architect's mind; trees lined it. This was not a place for ornamental, teased plantings. The scale of World's End would swallow them. Here his success would be judged by how invisible he could be. The blessings he provided must seem to have come from the hand of nature itself: each hedge, each tree must appear to have grown by its own easy wisdom.

He returned to the house just before dark, starving, pant legs muddy and flecked with flyaway grass. Partway up the drive he stopped. A woman stood at the top of the stairs, leashing a small white dog. He had not known there was anyone else in the house; he and Cale had eaten alone the night before, attended by a dour-faced butler who never looked up from the plates and dishes he carried.

His first impulse was to hide himself—absurd but imperative enough that he would have obeyed it if the woman, the girl, hadn't straightened up and seen him. She moved her eyes over him in a way that made him feel ashamed of every smudge and seed.

"Hello," she said. "I hope you brought a change of clothes for dinner?" She was young, at least a few years younger than the architect. She had wide and insincere eyes, and her frizzle of blond hair matched her frizzle of a dog. Her skin was like the surface of a vase. The architect had a sudden fierce urge to run his hand, with its dirt-stuffed fingernails, down that skin and mark it.

"Yes," he managed.

"Thank heaven for small favors," she said, and laughed a laugh that buzzed down his spine.

Not until dinner did the architect learn the girl's name: Becca, though Cale called her Becs, in a rough and doting way. She had just returned from visiting her cousins in Boston. Her mother seemed to be dead or otherwise absent. She had put on a dress of green silk, low and expertly cut enough that it seemed always just about to reveal more than it should, and said things that shocked the architect while she ate, impeccably. "I do wonder whether Lucy will *ever* get engaged. She likes men too much," she said. "And as for Carrie, well, Carrie looks like a camel." She dabbed at her lower lip with a fold of her napkin. The architect had never seen the gesture performed with such grace; he felt the awkwardness of his own grip on the silverware.

"Hmm," Cale said. He sliced his steak, lifted a neat section of it to his mouth, chewed. Then he turned to the architect. "Looked the place over, did you? What do you think?"

What the architect thought would have been difficult to put into words, and with Becca there, it seemed safer not to try. He gave a big and smiling nod.

"We'll talk over the particulars tomorrow morning before you go. I'm always in my study by five—never have thought you can get anything done in a day that doesn't begin while it's still dark. I've tried to convince Becs of that, but she likes her lie-ins."

"*Beauty* sleep," Becca said, touching the tips of her fingers to the white of her throat. "Those of us who leave the house, on occasion, need more of it."

A brief, stiff pause. Cale looked away. He took a swig of his wine and then thumped the goblet back to the table, so hard the architect expected the stem to break. "So, will we have to level the place out to put in the carriage roads?" he asked the architect, his voice louder than before.

"God, no," the architect said. "The roads should fit themselves to the land."

He had not meant to sound so dismissive. Becca turned her face to the architect for the first time, as if surprised not only by his addressing her father in such a tone but by his presence itself. "Whatever does that mean?" she said.

"They ought to *fit*." Under the weight of Becca's gaze, the architect fully grasped the foreignness of this territory. It occurred to him that building roads, which he had never done, was probably a complicated business, and that as confident as he felt of the essential rightness of this belief he was expressing, it was only a theoretical one. He tried to give his own voice a Cale-like boom. "Find the land's curves and settle in, bring them out. The way a dress fits a woman."

As soon as he said it he understood that he shouldn't have. He felt his face reddening. Though he might have gone on, said worse: the way a finger can learn a woman's shape by tracing her topography, and never lose the knowledge. That, at least, he had the sense not to say; he wasn't even quite sure of it. He had been with only two women, one a girl from back home, years before, and one the daughter of his landlord, and both would have laughed at him if he had ever attempted anything so fanciful as tracing them toe to chin with his finger.

Cale snorted. Becca raised her eyebrows. "Indeed," she said. She lifted her empty glass, which the butler promptly filled. Then she turned back to her father and began a tale of Lucy's scandalous exploits at a dinner party the Friday before. The architect was suffused with shame. He focused on eating silently, trying to keep his eyes on his plate. Yet he found that he could not stop looking at her.

ON THE TRAIN HOME the architect dreamed of green land, green, green silk.

HE SKETCHED AND PLANNED through the winter, using the drawings he'd made and the maps Cale had given him—fueled by Cale's checks, more money than he had ever before seen at one time. He spent the little he needed and deposited the rest in his bank account, unsure what to do with it.

Usually the architect hated winter in New York, the indoors season when the scant land that had been left exposed went dormant, when blackened piles of snow lingered and froze to the street corners in the poses of starving dogs. That year he didn't notice: he was in an eternal salt-smelling summer, parceling out World's End. The dividing up pleased him, for it let him accentuate the shape-shifting quality he loved in the place, the way it wore so many faces: a meadow house could have as its next-door neighbor a seaside house, which would abut a wooded house, all of them linked by the ribbony roads he would lay.

Those roads, though, were still worrisome. Not as an image—cutting across and banding the landscape, hemming the wildness in just enough to make it usable—but as a physical problem. He would have to make roads where now there were none. The idea opened a sort of queasy well within him at unpredictable times. In an effort to ease the feeling he moved out into the world, seeking men he knew from his handful of previous jobs, men with information. He found them in neighborhoods like the one where he'd been born, where the broken-boned buildings pressed together and held one another up as best they could. Here, in their cramped winter lairs, these men waited for spring and money to come again.

One December afternoon, the architect sat in the greasy-walled rooming house of a worker, the man who'd supervised the laying of walking paths through a courtyard the architect had designed the previous summer. He was twice the architect's age and had been a laborer for decades; he moved slowly, and his knuckles were red agonized knots. He was telling the architect about crushed stone and water-binding, and the architect was scribbling all of it into a notebook—trying to ignore the closeness of the air, the way the walls of the little room seemed to slump toward him, as if to catch and hold him there. Suddenly the worker stopped and squinted.

"What d'you want to know all this for?" he said.

"Just a job." The architect had decided ahead of time to be as indefinite as possible, afraid that word of his quest for information would somehow find its way back to Cale.

"Well, watch yourself. You do this wrong, the first good rain'll undo the whole thing for you." It had the sound of a warning meant for a child.

Afterward, needing a walk, the architect went to Central Park instead of straight home. The day was chill and wet, and almost no one was out. The most recent snowfall had been churned into the sand of the park's paths, making a slushy paste that seeped into his boots. Downed branches lay in hopeless tangles beneath the denuded, damp-barked trees. As the city found ways to shirk its costly upkeep, the park had begun a decline that felt irreversible. He didn't come here often anymore. Now he stood and gazed down the straight length of the Mall. A few people picked their way along its sides, heads down against the cold.

He'd been twelve the first time he'd seen this place—a while after the park's construction was complete. It had existed in what might as well have been a different city from his own, separated by space and money. On a still, hot midsummer day, the kind that made their tenement rooms unbearable, his brother, who'd have been fourteen, had told the architect to come with him, that he had a plan.

Outside was not, at first, much better than in. The

afternoon was gray and stifling, the streets crowded and ripe with horseshit and the breath of overheated people. His brother weaved between them.

"Where are we going?" the architect asked.

"You'll see."

They walked for a very long time, through parts of the city the architect had never seen. The faces and clothes of the people began to shift, to neaten, and yet they were still loud, still rushing. The buildings became taller, their edges crisper, and yet they were still buildings. The architect tried to look and to take things in; he understood that it might be a long time before he would see such things again. But a soft, panicked question began within him, growing louder as time stretched and they walked through more, always more, city streets: *Does it ever end?*

At last his brother had ducked into the park entrance. The architect had followed. He could remember even now the feel of that slip into space: the loosening of the air, the sudden quieting of the street noise. He felt himself quiet with it. When they reached the Mall, his older brother turned, so the architect did too. The lane was wide enough that a line of ten men could have joined their extended arms and walked forward together. He knew better than to stop and marvel, though, for they were surrounded again by other people—of a different sort than those on the streets outside. The ladies here wore expensive-looking dresses in watercolor shades and held the elbows of gentlemen. No one hurried or shouted. Instead they strolled and laughed mutedly, taking their time, as if the space around them were something they had paid for.

His brother had vanished up ahead. As the architect walked forward, it began to rain, a mist so fine it hung in the air. The rain wet the skin of his face, and suddenly there were breezes he had not felt before. There was a soft rustling on all sides as each group of walking people opened an umbrella. He

matched their pace, wondering where they were all going together. When the broad, tree-lined Mall ended at the top tier
of the Terrace, and the people around him parted to move
down the two halves of its divided staircase, he stopped and
leaned against the railing to watch them. The lake curved
away in front of him. Between the architect and the water, a
fountain splashed in the center of a brick-paved circle. The
crowd of people walked around it like something set to music.

The architect would later understand that with the Terrace,
Olmsted had been trying to lend his park the solidity of
tradition: the angel-topped fountain, staircase, and paved
promenade like something lifted out of the rear courtyard
of a European monarch. At twelve, he had known only that
he had found a new shape for his life. He'd stood, gathering
the courage he would need to descend the staircase and join
the people again. He was sure his brother was down there
already, nimbly picking pockets; the architect saw that this
was why he had brought them here. The architect did not
want to steal, though. It had never before occurred to him to
walk, as these people did, for the sheer sake of walking. But
he thought that he could stroll around and around until he
was one of them. As he'd looked he had tried to determine
how many times his tenement building—his entire crum-
bling block—could fit into the luxuriously cleared space
before him.

Within six months the measles would fall on his block
and carry from one crowded set of rooms to another just
as cooking smells and grime had always done. Within six
months, the brother he had followed here would be dead.

The architect looked around him, now, at the slushy
present-day Mall, and could not believe it had ever seemed
to hold such promise; he could see nothing but its ragged
aging. The thought of walking down to the Terrace, where
the stained fountain would be emptied for winter, suddenly

exhausted him. He turned to go. At home, he threw open his window, despite the cold, and diagrammed the macadam method, which he would use on his roads. He did this again and again. He diagrammed until he was confident he could have drawn a reasonable version, the respective widths of the layers in place, in full darkness.

THE ARCHITECT'S PLANS for the land itself remained free of the anxiety he had about the roads. When it came to the landscape, he felt, all winter, only a sort of greed that made it difficult to stop working. In addition to his big bird's-eye plan of the whole, he made separate sketches of each piece of World's End, considering how to bring out its truest self. The trick was to lay the emphasis in the right places and draw the eye to the form that was already there, just in need of un-earthing. The prize plot, the center from which all the others radiated, would be the peak of the hill where Cale had first brought him. The architect sketched it from several perspec-tives. He would just lip the breast of the hill with his road, which would then circle back behind the house (no more than a vague shadow in his mind, yet essential, the reason for all the rest), so that its double row of maples wouldn't obscure the view. But the house would not command the very crest. That would be given to a stand of pines he would plant, staggered so they would wear their grace artlessly. Seen from a distance, from every house on World's End, they would seem to lift the hill-line even farther into the sky. The architect drew with pencil, in thick, heavy lines, and smudged to show where the densest pockets of foliage would be, smudged with his fingers. His studio became dappled in gray fingerprints. Their concentration, greatest at the desk pressed up against the room's biggest window, mapped the way he spent his hours.

But he did not always concentrate fully on the drawing. As he sketched each plot, as its form came together in his mind, he began to imagine—so clearly that daydreaming was too pale a word—laying Becca Cale down on that slip of land and making love to her. In the meadow, where the grasses would be tall enough to wall off the space around them, where long and fragrant strands of mown hay would tangle in her fuzzy hair until he combed them roughly away with his fingers, where they would begin to feel the grasshoppers' hum in their skin, in their veins, in their tongues. On the tidal marsh, the glossy, impossibly vivid grass like the pelt of some animal and the rich, dark, heavy-smelling mud like its hide, where the wet would leach through their clothes, where it would slick their lips, where he could suck water salty as tears from the collar of her dress. Under a gracious old oak he remembered, whose limbs arched up and bowed down again to form a kind of room, spreading shade below like the most expensive of carpets; the grass there would store the cool at its roots so that Becca would be the warmest thing he could feel. On the topmost ground of that crowning hill, all of World's End at their feet, where there would be nothing but space around them, where he could imagine that he felt the eyes of the distant city on them as they moved.

If he had been asked, the architect would have said that these visions were neither likely nor impossible. His dreams had so far led him forward—starting with the moment three years earlier when, working on a bricklaying crew, he had muttered to the rich man who had hired them that he was putting his wall in the wrong place, and the rich man had heard. He knew his dreams of World's End were different from the others; he just wasn't sure what this difference meant. At the finish of his imagined wanderings with Becca, sponging his own gray fingerprints, like feathery bruises, off his body, he felt a guilt and doubt that were new to him. But again and again the fingerprints returned.

AS THE TIME DREW NEARER to implement his plans, to see if real materials could hold the shapes from his sketches, the architect's days took on a strung-tight feeling. He returned to World's End when the ground thawed, ready, thanks to the winter's furious work, to begin. He had the aggravating suspicion that Cale had no idea what a feat this was. Or perhaps Cale did not make a habit of openly acknowledging the feats of those he was paying. Cale was covering all of his expenses, and the architect knew he should have been content; still, he could not quite bring himself to welcome the nod that met each particular of his plans. It was too much like the nod Cale gave his butler.

On his fourth morning back, the architect was on his stomach in the grass beside the new-cut beginnings of the first road, checking the camber, when he turned his head to find himself suddenly face-to-feet with Becca: a slightly lifted skirt and a pair of boots, tiny and so sharp looking he was surprised they didn't punch right through the turf. He hadn't yet seen her since his return or even worked up the courage to ask Cale where she was, afraid that his voice would betray him.

He hefted himself to his feet and only then raised his eyes to Becca's face.

"Certainly becoming one with all this, aren't you?" she said. "Down in the very dirt."

The workmen tipped their hats to her. The architect glanced back in their direction; until now he had mostly forgotten them in his preoccupation with the road. "Camber looks good," he told them. "Why don't you all have a break."

"All right, boss," the foreman said, but it had the wrong sound, and his expression was almost a smirk. At least the workers did as the architect had asked, dropped their rakes and shovels and faded back toward the trees, where they had stored their lunch pails and cigarettes.

The architect turned to Becca and tried to brush off his

front and gesture to the road at the same time. "I was checking the angle. It has to be right or the runoff will wash it out when it rains."

Becca smoothed her wind-mussed puff of fringe with a gloved hand. Then she minced—constrained by those little boots, that narrow though many-layered skirt—around the place where the road's progress ended, eyeing the freshly laid gravel. When she stopped, she and the architect stood on opposite sides. It was a strange thing for him to see her after all their intimacies in his imagination. He had spent hours in his head with his skin touching hers.

Finally she looked up again. "Well, I do hope I'm not interrupting. I had a bit of time before Mr. Poynter's due. We're to go driving—I promised him." He could tell from the way she dropped the name that it was an impressive one. He imagined a thickset man with a fancy coat and a face like a pocket watch, full of buried, crisp, malevolent ticking.

"Right," the architect said, to say something.

"I only thought I'd come to see all of the progress." Her mouth twitched with a small smile. "And now I've seen it all, haven't I?"

"We've just started," he said, stung. But she had already turned toward the house, and she did not look back. The architect caught a glimpse of the circle of workmen, by the trees, and hated the knowingness with which they all turned away from him.

THE WORK, THOUGH, BEGAN to go very well. Better, the architect understood, than he'd had any right to expect. He clung to this; it dulled the memory of Becca's scorn. So did the way the workmen's amusement seemed to diminish as the roads advanced. At the end of each day's work, there was a stretch of road that had not been there at the start, as if it had been unfurled like fabric from some invisible bolt. The roads lay soft as cloth, too, dipping and rising with the land beneath, showcasing all of that stopped motion.

Even the large plantings were underway before long, for Cale proved easy to convince on the matter of mature trees instead of saplings for some locations. The architect faced him across his wide, ink-stained plane of a desk and explained things. He told Cale what it would cost but that if he chose the cheaper saplings, he would never see the architect's design as it was meant to be seen, that the men who would witness its full realization hadn't yet been born.

As he listened, Cale's lips took on a pinch. He didn't seem to like thinking about these men who would live on after him. "When you put it that way."

The architect produced the piece of paper. Cale pinned it to the desktop and signed with a flourish, delighting, perhaps, in taking for himself some part of a future that should not by rights have belonged to him.

The architect watched with a feeling of triumph. "We should begin talking about the builders for the houses too."

Cale put his pen down and pushed the paper toward the architect. His hand lingered on the desk. "Good to do business here again," he said. "This used to be in my office in the city—bought a new one the year before the Great Fire and moved this one out here. The replacement was made specially for me, in Italy. Cinders now. But this one's an old battlefield." With his gaze on its surface, he did have the dreamy look of some aged general. A disquieting image came to the architect: Cale, arranging toy soldiers in rows on this desktop, making boyish noises of war with his mouth. Positioning the fallen, at the end of the game, in ink spills meant for pools of blood.

"Sir? The houses?"

Cale waved a hand. "Not yet. Let's take care of the roads and the trees, for now."

So the architect contacted his suppliers and ordered

larch and maple and tulip, oak and ash and catalpa. They arrived prone and trussed up, bound giants; once planted they sprung into strong-limbed life. Only a few didn't take. The rest were eager to play their role in defying time. The architect ministered to them all like a physician and found, at the end of most days, that his hands were sticky with their mingled sap.

Once he'd washed up, he ate his dinners at the Cale house. Becca was often absent, visiting her cousins or friends for weeks at a time. This didn't bother the architect. She was more real to him when she was away. The days when she was there, he saw her only briefly and usually from a distance, at about midday, when she would walk her dog down the flat stretch of road that led to the main hill at World's End and then turn around where the ground began to rise. The nights when she was at dinner, chattering loudly right across the table and yet as separate as if locked in a display case, were the ones that drove the architect out to the land the next morning, to clutch up whole fistfuls of grass and dirt when the workmen weren't watching and assure himself that he still had the power of grasping, of touch.

One afternoon two months into the work, a sudden and furious spring rainstorm sent a muddy stream of runoff cascading down a hillside in a way that no one had expected. The main road lay right in its path. The architect ran to the roadside, where there was nothing to do but stand with his foreman and wait. Even above the din of the rain, he could hear his own blood in his ears. This—the angry torrent of water—was real motion, come to attack the sculpture of motion the architect had carved into the land. The water wanted to do its own carving.

They watched as it pounded at the road. Yet it was the water, minute after minute, that lost its shape where the two met. It ceased to be a waterfall and hugged the road's contours instead, slipping down the hill, the gentlest of travelers.

Finally the foreman turned to him. He had to yell to be heard through the downpour. "Seems all right."

The architect felt a swoop of joy so violent it threatened to upend him. He was going to manage this, he thought. Every surrounding beauty seemed to him something he himself had summoned, down to the fresh-watered smell of growth in the air, the strength of the oaks above them, and most of all this graveled stretch of road, which would not yield. This place would be equal to his vision for it; he was standing inside a world he had plucked full-bodied from his own head. He looked to the top of the central hill, hazy through the rain, where the pines he had planted stood against the sky like soft, dark streaks of paint. When the project was finished, completely finished, once the admiring world had been let in and his name was on everyone's lips, he would find a way to walk with Becca to that hilltop. From there he could show her, explain the shape of what he had done, point to its features and watch her attention follow. She would see him then. She would have to. For he had turned himself inside out here, poured everything he had across this land, and there it would be, spread before her.

SOON IT WAS SUMMER, and the roads and the trees were almost done. The architect took satisfaction in going out to the land each morning to find them still in their proper places. Yet the work with the roads and trees was really all that could be accomplished before Cale chose a builder and began to line up the buyers—and Cale seemed in no hurry to do this. He didn't say anything outright about wanting to wait, but days passed and nothing was decided. He'd taken to coming out to World's End in the early evenings, to check on the status of things, he said, but once there he only paced the roads with his eyes on the sky. The architect brought the houses up often—during these walks, when he'd run to catch up with Cale, and during their morning meetings. He'd found several good builders' names, and he dropped them. Each time Cale would grunt.

After some weeks of this, the architect came back from one of his consultations with Cale to find his workmen sprawled on the grass in the sun, hats over their eyes, smoking. "What's happening here?" He was too startled to be angry. "It's ten-thirty. Two hours till break."

Several of the men laughed and got up, slapping their palms together to get the grass off, throwing their cigarettes away. But the foreman merely shifted his hat back so that he could see the architect and propped himself on an elbow. "We're having a rest," he said.

The architect motioned to the forked stretch of road beside them. "That right branch needs leveling this morning, all the way up past the rise."

"Didn't see the hurry, I guess."

Quiet fell then, as the men watched their reclining foreman and the architect. The architect looked away, down the left branch, the one they'd finished weeks earlier. At the trees' roots, the road's edges, the ground that had been cut was already healing over with low creeping greenery. Its harsh lines were softening. Overhead in the new branches, birds chattered to each other. The architect tried to think of the right thing to say. The only hurry in finishing the right branch of the road was to enable building materials to be brought in for the houses on the north side. It was one of the last jobs left on the prebuilding list. Suddenly everything around him felt heavy and inert, as if he had put a whole elaborate circuitry in place here, but had neglected for too long to give it a heart.

He told the workmen to get moving and left them that way, though who knew what they would be doing when he returned. He made himself go slowly and calmly back to Cale's house. Their meeting that morning had been in Cale's study, but when the architect climbed the stairs he found the door open, the room empty. Parker, the butler, was clearing the glasses he and Cale had left. "Where is he?" the architect asked.

"Mr. Cale often spends the late morning in his sitting room," Parker said, indicating the hallway with his heavy-lidded, disapproving eyes.

The architect thanked him and was gone and down the hall before Parker could say anything else. He knocked at the door and opened it. There was Cale, in a small, dark, blood-colored hole of a room, reclined on a sofa in a silk dressing gown as red as the rest, so that on first glance he blended into the brocade.

"I thought you were Parker," Cale said.

The architect waited, unsure whether this was a dismissal. The room was too warm and smelled of heavy drapery. He could not have imagined there was a room this small in Cale's house. Cale sat up a little, pulling the gown's folds closed at his throat, a modest woman's gesture. "Sometimes, when the morning's business is over," he said, "I come in here. To be comfortable for a while. Sometimes a man deserves to be comfortable."

The architect nodded, trying to keep his face blank. An embroidered peacock twined itself across the back cushion of Cale's sofa, so blue against the red background that it looked poisonous. Its neck made a full S-shape, and its single eye, too large for its tiny head, seemed fixed on the architect. He forced himself to look away, but there was nowhere else to rest his gaze. Everywhere he looked, a different pattern: writhing vines on the deep red walls, on the curtains gold stitching, gold paint like scales on the ebony sideboard, the ceiling three tiers deep and thickly painted, the floor an intricate parquet topped with an Oriental carpet. And Cale himself, of course, in his robe.

"I only came back because I realized—I saw that I haven't

been clear. About the houses," the architect said. "Starting the houses. We need to begin the plans now. I've done all I can do until then."

"Well," said Cale. "Why don't you go on back home, then, if you're done."

The word *home* from Cale's mouth somehow brought to mind not the architect's current apartment in New York but the one in which he had grown up, as if Cale were sending him back to the tenement he had come from. He was finding it difficult to breathe. "Go home? I don't understand."

Cale stood and strode the few paces to the curtained window, his back to the architect. "I'll write you when I'm ready," he said.

"But the land is ready *now*."

Cale reached out and parted the cloth, letting sunlight flood the room. The red of the walls turned brighter, deeper, in the light, and the architect had to blink against it. "Not for you to decide, is it? You've built your roads. I've paid you for them." Cale put his other hand out, palm flat to the window, looking at the view. There was World's End, the architect saw, through the glass.

Cale took his hand away after a moment, and the fabric closed off the light and the view again. He turned to the architect, a faceless, dim figure now with arms extended, the sleeves of his dressing gown hanging like injured wings. "I did think I wanted to do it. The place would have made me a fortune. No one else saw it, they all said it was too far out from the city, but I knew. Bennett said you'd be sure to leave lots of room, and you have done good work. I've just changed my mind."

He might have used the same words to change a dinner engagement or an order for a new jacket. The peacock on the sofa seemed to underscore the architect's humiliation with its mocking eye. He knew what the bird would say if it could speak: *You didn't honestly believe any of it could be yours, did you?*

"Why?" the architect managed. He hated how small and soft the word sounded.

Cale dropped his gaze, and for a moment the architect thought he wouldn't answer. Then: "Do you remember the Great Fire?" Cale said. "I suppose you were only a child then, and maybe they didn't talk so much about it outside Boston. But I was there that night, in my office. Watched it from my window, coming for me through the dark. Coming from a couple of different directions at once, jumping right across the roofs, like somebody'd laid a nice path for it."

In spite of himself, the architect found that he could see this. The fire sprung up readily in his mind.

"Took me a minute to understand I should run, and a minute was almost too long. It was the roofs that did it. Damn death-trap wooden roofs all those fools around me used on their buildings."

The architect watched the red-orange line of flame flying from roof to roof, so little space between. He had watched in the same way that terrible week when first his youngest brother and then his sister and then finally his older brother had caught the measles; he had seen the sickness leap from one to the next, agile as fire, and flush his siblings with rash and fever. He remembered how their mother's face had tightened as she hardened herself. How the rest of them were sleeping on the floor, out of the shared bed, but every-one had known that it wouldn't matter—his sister and his older brother had been sleeping on the floor too before they fell ill. Every night of the week it took them to die, in that stale and fetid room, he had listened to the swampy sounds of their breathing in the bed, turned his face to the wall in the dark, and tried to pretend that the air in his mouth wouldn't kill him. He unlearned all the love he had ever felt for any of them during those hours. To get free of that room he would have razed their whole tenement—with his family inside it, if necessary. In his mind, he'd flattened that building, the one next to it, the one next to that, and spread a lavish dream-canopy of distance all around himself.

"I like World's End how it is now," Cale said. "I like it all empty, the way you've done it. Somehow with everything you've added, it feels emptier than it did before. Feels like I'm the only man in the world when I walk there."

Of course it did. The architect closed his eyes.

"I'll send the last check to New York, shall I?"

The architect opened his eyes again. He did not hit Cale, as he wanted to. He only nodded, and when Cale held out his hand, he shook it. "Fine," he said.

The architect left the red room. He went down the stairs and out the front door, then turned back, for a moment, to face the house. It had the look of something made of marble, permanently sealed. Though the door had only just shut behind him, he could not believe he had ever been inside at all.

There were things to be done now. Workmen to inform and dismiss, belongings to gather, a journey back to New York to arrange. He thought of these things, and yet somehow he continued to stand with his hands in his pockets partway down the static hill that was the house's pedestal.

At the tip of the road, he saw Becca—walking with her dog in the direction of World's End. He came back to himself in a warm rush. He ran. She was not difficult to overtake. She heard him coming and turned her head, raising a hand to shade her view.

"My, aren't you in a hurry," she said when he reached her. Her lips curved, pink as her pink walking dress. All that concentration of color: she looked covered in a layer of enamel. He wondered if Mr. Poynter had taken her driving this morning, run his fingers over those lips, called her lovely. He himself wanted to peel the dress off her and see the color of the skin beneath. He wanted this so much and so recklessly, all at once, that he had to put his hands back in his pockets and ball up his fists to stop himself.

"I hoped I might join you," he said.

"It would appear," she said, "that you have." She began walking again, and he fell into step beside her. The dog trotted in front of them, down the very middle of the road, uninterested in its surroundings. To keep himself calm, the architect watched its bobbing tail.

They came to the entrance of World's End. As they passed through the stone gate, the architect felt the change, as always, in his lungs, which seemed to ease and expand in the new air. The main road stretched before them, lined on both sides by oaks that laced the sun into patterns on the gravel—a road so beautiful it might go anywhere, he thought. He snuck a glance at Becca's smooth, expressionless face and extended his arms to indicate what he had made. "I wanted large trees for the entrance," he said. "For a sense of grandeur. And shade for the cool in the summer, of course."

"Jouette!" Becca said. The little dog had stopped to groom itself; when she yanked it forward it toppled, then righted itself again. "Well, I must say, I never mind the heat. I'm sick to death of this chill we've had in the evenings. Mr. Poynter always has to bring a blanket for our drives."

The walk stretched forward with too many possibilities; the architect could hardly concentrate for considering them. He could take her first to the sea, or first to the meadow. Or the main hill first. Yes. In any case, they were almost there. The hill rose in front of them, obscuring the city view they would have from its height. "I've been hoping to show all of this to you for some time," he told her.

But Becca had stopped with her face in shadow and her pink skirt lit up by the sun. She was tugging on Jouette's leash again, though the dog was still going forward. She was tugging it back.

The architect realized with panic that they were just where he'd watched Becca turn around so many times before on her midday walks.

"A little farther," he said. "Just up this hill is the real view. You can see everything."

"Many thanks, I'm sure. I'm afraid I haven't much enthusiasm for climbing hills."

"But you wouldn't even have to go all the way up. Part of the way only—half, a third, and you could see the city past the trees. You could see the ocean. The land, how different it all is now. Please."

She'd begun to move away. If he could not make her go up that hill to see, it would be as if everything that was visible from the top had never existed. His hand was on her before he even knew what he was doing. His fingers had closed around her wrist. Too hard, he knew. "Come with me."

She stopped moving. Her eyes dropped to his hand. The shock on her face was more genuine than any other feeling he'd seen there—as if this, the touch of his skin, were the most brutal thing that had ever happened to her. "What are you *doing*?" Her voice was high with alarm.

Jouette began a frantic yipping.

This was the moment to which the architect would return, again and again, in the years that followed. It would come to seem to him that there were things he might have done next. He might have lifted her and run up the hill. He might have tightened his grip enough to bruise, to show her that he could. While she was right there in front of him, while his hand was on her, he might have found some way of testing his idea that her behavior was only a shell over the truth of her—that if her veins were opened, loamy earth might spill out in clumps, that if he sniffed deeply enough at the roots of her hair, he might smell the sea.

Instead his grip loosened. She tugged her arm away. He sought a mark, a smudge, some evidence that he had touched

her, and could find none. He watched her leave him in a
swish of pink skirts, her back to his great unfinished work.

The architect would go home, and eventually he would
marry his landlord's daughter. She would make him happy
in a slowly accreting kind of way. Over the years, he would
achieve much of which he would feel proud. These accom-
plishments he stacked in rows in his mind, hiding the ground
beneath. Nothing could change the shape of that ground—
but the ground of his real life he paced with confidence. He
walked beside his clients through their land, explaining to
them what they should see, and when he and his wife went
down a street together, he would take her arm and hold her
warm against his side.

It was only in the space just before sleep that he returned,
again and again, to the short walk he had not taken. Each
time, the main hill of World's End took shape before him,
Becca beside him, and he set out. Twenty more steps. He
could imagine taking every one of them. Thirty, perhaps.
Then she would have seen.

GRANNA

In the wake of the end of things with Adam, a good and generous man, Teresa felt the need to do something self-evidently good and generous. Adam had made her feel incapable of giving. She would show him giving. She called her older sister Deb and said, "Let's take Granna up north."

"*Granna?*"

But there were tried, true ways to force Deb to override her better judgment. Teresa blew a gentle puff of air into the phone.

"I just think," she said, "that it's the right thing."

When they pulled up to the retirement home where they had stashed Granna five years earlier, she was there on the bench out front, hands crossed in the lap of her high-waisted silken dress, waiting for them, looking very, very old. *Where do*

you even get dresses like that anymore? Deb had said once, years
ago. Until Deb mentioned them, Teresa would never have
thought to wonder about the dresses, any more than she
would have wondered about Granna's own particular skin.

"Yikes," said Deb's daughter, Ellie, from the backseat, as
Granna rose, squinted at the car, and began to come slowly
toward it, shuffling in her Band-Aid–colored shoes. Ellie was
nine now. Teresa hadn't seen her since Christmas. During
the car ride, she had displayed a new knack for saying aloud
the very thought that had been in Teresa's head, too, but
that she never would have voiced, so that being with Ellie was
like being stripped naked before herself.

"Hush," Deb told Ellie. Then, "Where are her bags? Doesn't
she have any bags? I'll go ask." Granna stopped when Deb
reached her. Deb put her hand on Granna's arm and mur-
mured something while Granna looked past her, fixing her
milky eyes on Teresa's face.

Teresa remembered those eyes' former sharpness. When
tiny ants had overrun Granna's kitchen in the summers of
Teresa's childhood, Granna had spotted them, even from
across the room, and crushed each individually, with books,
the bottoms of her dainty coffee cups, her heel, her naked
fingers. She used to eye Teresa's outfits and send her upstairs
to change if she found the smallest stain or stray thread. The
scrutiny had felt frightening and wondrous. No one else
in Teresa's life had ever seen her so clearly. When Teresa
was eleven or twelve, though, dimness began to settle over
Granna; Teresa's mother had said she was "slowing down." So
they'd left her behind. Deb and Teresa stopped taking their
summer trips with Granna to the line of cabins in the Vermont
woods near where she had grown up, and they visited her less
and less often. Eventually they'd taken Granna's whole life
and dumped it here, in this small, gray place.

Teresa was going to let that life out into the air again. She was going to carry Granna right back into a family Vermont trip, as if those trips had never stopped.

But her sense of the trip's rightness was wilting, confronted with Granna in the flesh. Granna lowered herself into the front seat of the car while Deb fetched her forgotten suitcase. She faced straight ahead as they drove away. Her hands lay on her knees like abandoned things, the knuckles swollen and pearly as bulbs. Teresa hadn't managed to remember her quite this ancient. With Deb and Ellie, Teresa had visited last year and sat with her for an hour in her room at the home, that space overfull of the table lamps, ceramic figurines of women in ball gowns, and patterned pillows Teresa remembered from Granna's house—as if someone had taken that house, with everything still inside it, and squeezed and squeezed. Granna had sipped from a glass of water, spoken a few times. Now she said nothing. Nobody said anything. Granna watched the road. Teresa imagined Adam's beautifully expressive eyes on her, rich with disappointment: *Is this helping, Ter?*

"It's so good to see you, Granna," Teresa said. She tried not to speak too slow or too loud. "I've been looking forward to this."

Granna smiled.

Deb leaned forward to cup Granna's shoulder with her palm. "We all have, Granna," she said. Ellie rested her cheek against the window.

They stopped halfway, at a rest-area bathroom. Teresa and Deb walked on either side of Granna with her arms in their hands; beneath Teresa's fingers, Granna's skin rolled loose over the bones in her elbow. Teresa wasn't sure how hard to grip. She looked to Deb for clues, but Deb was distracted, talking to Ellie behind them, telling her that she couldn't have a soda from the vending machine, there was seltzer in the car. What must it be like, Teresa wondered, to have to experience the world in such a fragile body? You would evaluate the direction of every step, if walking was this hard. Yet here Granna was, stepping off into the wilderness with them. Well, she could sit safely on the porch of their cabin for the whole trip, breathing in the fresh air. Teresa would bring her every last thing she needed, before she even realized she needed it: plates of food, cups of orange juice and tea on skillfully balanced trays.

Teresa and Deb sparred over who would pay for their drive-through dinner, and Teresa won, handing money through the window while Deb was still grappling with her wallet. Granna removed and ate only the top bun of her Quarter Pounder. By the time they turned in to the pitted drive that led to Sanderson's Mountain Cabins it was almost dark, and Granna had fallen gently asleep with her chin tipped up toward the roof of the car.

Time had not been kind to Sanderson's Mountain Cabins, or else Teresa's memory had been too kind. Each of the ten sad, white cabins seemed to be ailing in a different way: a missing shutter, a patchy roof, a tilted front step. They sat in their half circle with tragic patience, as if they'd gathered here to await improvement without any hope that it was actually coming. When Teresa parked, Granna opened her eyes and cleared her throat with a pebbly sound.

On her way back to the car with their cabin keys, #7 for Teresa and Granna, #8 for Deb and Ellie, Teresa thought she saw a shadowy, sinuous something twist its way from the corner of the porch and off into the bushes, where it rustled in the leaves. She jumped and hoped the others hadn't seen. A squirrel, probably, that her mind had made larger and darker.

When Ellie opened the car door she said gleefully, "Scaredy-cat, Aunt Terry!"

They dispersed and unpacked. Granna leaned against the headboard of her bed with legs extended and shoes still on, placid face lovely in the light of the old boxy television. It was impossible to tell from her expression what she was thinking, or whether she was thinking anything at all.

"Are you comfortable?" Teresa asked.

"Oh yes," Granna said.

Deb knocked at the door then, and asked Teresa if she'd come for a walk. Teresa wasn't sure about leaving Granna, but she could tell from Deb's voice that it wasn't really a request. They took the path that led from the back of the cabins toward the stream and swimming hole they'd loved as kids. The air had a dark chill. Deb kept her flashlight trained on the ground right in front of them. Like everything else here, the swimming hole proved slighter in all ways than Teresa remembered—its sound less a babble than a slow seeping—though it did still have the leafy, soaked smell she would have known anywhere. Deb swatted at a mosquito on her leg. "I think," she said, "that we should consider a change of plans."

"Why?"

Deb widened her eyes. "Seriously? I know this is a hard time for you and everything, but we can't just stay out here in the woods in the middle of nowhere for a whole week. With an old lady. What are we going to do with her?"

"Where did you think we were going? You've been here."

"I don't remember it being so . . . " She extended her hands and held up the thick blackness, as if measuring it.

Teresa was not going to admit defeat on this, her project of goodness. "We promised Granna and Ellie a vacation, Deb."

"Ellie? Ellie is going to kill me if I make her stay here."

"You'll see," Teresa said. "Just wait. It will all look better in the morning." They were hardly going to pile back in the car and drive through the night. Ring the bell at the retirement home at two in the morning and speed away, leaving Granna blinking on the doorstep and gripping her suitcase like a foundling.

Deb sighed. "We'll talk more tomorrow. It's not like it makes sense to leave now," she said, letting it be known that sense, and not Teresa, had convinced her. All their lives Deb had been sensible. In between their visits, Teresa always forgot how maddening this could be. Now Deb turned her back and started down the path.

Granna had already tucked herself into bed by the time Teresa returned, and her breathing was soft and even. She'd left the overhead light on. Teresa switched it off, turned on her dim bedside lamp. She went about her bedtime preparations in shadow, giving herself a splinter in the side of her thigh when she brushed against the raw wood of the bathroom door. In bed, she read two pages of the book Adam had given her for her most recent birthday—thirty-one—before realizing she was hearing the words in his voice. She turned off the light.

Last month, Adam had looked at her in a considering kind of way and said, "I just don't know if you're a *mother*."

They were talking, as they'd begun to do (though only after a long time—maybe that should have been a sign), about getting married, about children. It had taken a minute for the hurt of the words to hit Teresa. Initially, she'd just felt confused. Of course she wasn't a mother, not yet.

"It's just something I feel about you," he said. "You, and being maternal."

What was there to say in response? Teresa supposed she could have told him he didn't seem very paternal to her either, but both of them would have known it was a lie. She wondered how it happened that some people just turned out obviously better than others. Yet it seemed terrible of him not to have given her a chance, that largest of all possible chances, to transcend the way she seemed.

Teresa lay very still in her bed, not sleeping but trying to sound like an asleep person, trying to not wake Granna. She realized, though, that Granna was indeed awake. She heard the rustling of the covers, and then a watchful silence. Teresa stayed silent herself by instinct. She cracked open her eyes to see Granna moving not toward the bathroom but toward their cabin's front door, still in her nightgown. Granna pulled the door open and closed it quietly behind her.

Teresa sat up in bed. So Granna had stepped out. To do what? She waited to see if Granna would come right back, which of course she would have to, because where was there, in this place, for a ninety-year-old woman to go? When a minute passed and she didn't return, Teresa went outside. Granna was picking her way through the parking lot with the caution of someone walking on ice. Teresa advanced. She would lay a hand on Granna's arm, a gentle, nonstartling hand. But then a crane fly, trailing its long thready legs, brushed Teresa's lips tenderly, and she gave a quiet shriek. Granna turned around.

"I'm getting some air," Granna said. Teresa thought there was a plaintive note in her voice. "I want to look at the moon."

"Let me come with you."

"No thank you."

I come or you're not going, Teresa wanted to say. But she wasn't Granna's mother. "Only for a few minutes?" Teresa asked.

Granna nodded.

Teresa returned to her bed to wait. While she was waiting she fell asleep. She woke to daylight and Granna propped up in bed.

"Good morning," Granna said. "Didn't you have a nice long beauty sleep."

Teresa sat up, raked at her hair.

Granna swung her feet to the floor. "Shall we go find the others? See about breakfast? I'm *hungry*." She clapped her hands, making Teresa flinch.

When Deb opened their cabin door, Granna spread her arms and said, "Happy new day!"

"What's with you?" Ellie said, the exact thing Teresa had been thinking, again.

"The air up here agrees with me," Granna said.

On their way to the car, Deb gave Teresa a look behind Granna's back. Teresa shrugged.

They drove down the road to a diner with plastic menus full of unappetizing photos of the food. Before deciding, Granna rested a longing fingertip on the waffles, the breakfast hash, and breathed in deep, as if trying to catch their scent. When the waitress took her order, Granna said more words together than Teresa had heard from her in the whole of the previous evening. Rye toast, not white; well done, but not too well done; hot sauce brought to the table, please. Everyone but Ellie tried not to stare while Granna devoured her eggs. "This tastes so good!" Granna said. A clump of egg clung to the front of her dress. Deb leaned forward to brush it off and Granna swatted her hand away and did it herself.

"What shall we do next?" Granna asked as they pulled back into Sanderson's Mountain Cabins.

Teresa hadn't thought there'd be a need to do much of anything on this trip. She had figured Granna's days would consist of naps, long naps. Deb must have had the same idea; she said, "Maybe a little rest?"

Granna laughed. "What would we be resting from? Let's go to the swimming hole."

Teresa—and, she was sure, Deb too—thought of tree roots and slippery rocks, filtered and insufficient forest light.

"I used to go there when I was a girl, did I ever tell you that?"

Teresa couldn't remember that Granna ever had, no. She wanted to get Granna back to their cabin and make her sit down, recover from whatever this was, and turn back into someone Teresa understood. "That's a long walk, Granna," she said. "Let's see how you're doing in a little bit."

"I want to go swimming," Ellie said.

"Not now, Ellie," Deb told her.

Teresa stole a glance at her niece in the rearview mirror. Ellie's forehead was creasing, her mouth opening, as she readied herself to throw a fit about this, if necessary. When children wanted things, they wanted them so desperately.

"Let's do it," Teresa said. "Why not?" She smiled at Granna and threw a wild grin at Ellie.

"Good," said Granna.

"Okay," Ellie said warily.

While they were all swimming, maybe Teresa would splash her, or push her head playfully under, and win her over.

"Why not? You're really asking that?" Deb said. But she shook her head and closed her eyes for a moment instead of arguing further. Deb, Teresa thought, was getting tired.

So they set off. Ellie crashed ahead through brambles that scored red scratches across her skinny legs, which were like line drawings of the legs she would have someday. Teresa and Deb hovered behind Granna while she walked. They kept their hands outstretched toward her, as if they'd just set a vase down precariously. Slow but oddly steady, Granna advanced. Sweat droplets beaded up on the back of her neck, above the collar of that same silk dress, which seemed to be all she had brought, apart from her nightgown. When they arrived at the swimming hole, she seated herself on a rock, swiveling her hips from side to side to get comfortable. She began removing her shoes.

"Granna, what are you doing?" Deb asked.

"Wading!"

Before either Deb or Teresa had worked out a response, she was indeed standing in the water, flexing her fish-white toes in the stream's current, smiling up at the trees. "My lord," Granna whispered, "that feels wonderful."

Ellie wended her way upstream to where the river curved into oblivion. Deb looked after her, face straining with the effort to attend to these divergent worries. "Ellie!" she called, "Ellie, don't go where I can't see you, okay?" When Ellie didn't stop, Deb glanced once more at Granna and followed her daughter.

Teresa sized Granna up, decided she looked stable enough, took off her own sandals, and waded to a rock that would let her sit with her feet in the water. The rock, which had looked flat, turned out to be a sneaky poker. Teresa remembered how Granna had watched her swim here, on their trips years earlier, while Deb had tried to find a patch of bank sunny enough for tanning. Diving to the bottom of the swimming hole, probably fifteen feet deep, had seemed to Teresa an irresistible challenge. Every summer she'd gotten nosefuls of mud-tasting water during her first efforts and burst into tears. But she'd always managed it in the end by forcing herself a little deeper each time she failed, even as her lungs burned. She grabbed rocks from the bottom as proof for herself of what had been accomplished, and when she finally came up with them, Granna would applaud. For years, Teresa had kept those rocks in a line on her dresser. If she did manage to have a child someday, she wondered if she would ever understand that child the way Granna had understood her.

Granna turned her eyes on Teresa now. "You're old," she said.

Teresa let out a bark of laughter—Granna, with her short dry white hair and her face like moist lined paper, was calling her old. Except it suddenly seemed that there were fewer lines than before around Granna's eyes, and something newly elastic in the way her mouth moved.

"Well, not old really," Granna allowed, "but not young. I remember that you were young. Where's that man you had? What was his name?"

"Adam."

"*Adam*," Granna repeated, with the satisfaction of finding a lost object. "Why isn't he here?"

Primly, Teresa told her, "We aren't together anymore."

Granna pursed her lips. Teresa tried to decide what her grandmother might say next. Granna began to wade toward her, positioning each foot with deliberation on the rocks. The water made licking sounds against her shins. She came close enough for touching, and then she touched: bent to put her hands on Teresa's folded knees. She leaned in.

"That's a sad thing," she said. "What will you do about it?"

THEY PLAYED MINI GOLF LATER that afternoon, at a place Ellie had spotted on their way to breakfast. "I'm starting over," Ellie declared, when she sent her ball into the sand trap with her fourth impatient stroke.

"Sure!" Teresa said.

"You'll remember that you fudged it, at the end, and if you do well, it won't mean as much," said Granna, lining up her own shot.

"Whatever. Do over." Ellie moved her ball back to the start.

They ate dinner at the course's burger stand, Teresa scuffing her shoes across the balding Astroturf under their picnic table. She bought them all ice-cream cones on the way home. While the others sat on the front porch of Deb and Ellie's cabin to eat theirs, she crammed hers into her mouth as she snuck away, around the back of her own cabin, to call Adam. She had known she would call Adam all afternoon.

His greeting sounded weary.

"Just wanted to say hello," Teresa told him. She lowered herself to sit on the ground and leaned back against the cabin, sucking the last ice-cream stickiness off her fingers. "From Vermont. I'm in Vermont."

She could hear him trying to figure out if there was any way to avoid asking and deciding there wasn't. "What are you doing up there?"

Here it was, Teresa's chance for her big reveal, her proof of selflessness. "Remember how my Granna used to take us to spend summers up here when I was a kid? I started thinking—maybe we owe her that now. So Deb and I brought Granna and Ellie up for a few days. To give them both a nice time."

She'd imagined that when she told Adam this, his head would fill with pictures: herself with her hair bandannaed up fetchingly, Granna's hand tight with gratitude on hers, Ellie frolicking around them, Deb an incidental smudge in the periphery. But even she couldn't see these pictures anymore. Her head was full of Adam, who, she knew, she somehow just knew, was biting his nails. "Well good for you, Ter," he said.

"What?" she said.

"Nothing. Sounds great." *Nothing*, or *never mind*, Adam had often said, changing his mind after starting to say what he really thought about her. The time she took a little green enameled Japanese vase from their friend's house while they were over for dinner, just slipping it into her pocket while no one was looking. The time she let her boss think it was her office mate's fault that they'd lost an account. A hundred other, littler moments when she'd proved herself small.

"Give Granna a big hug from me, okay?" Adam said now.

"Why are you being like this?" Teresa asked him.

"Like what?"

Like a person who doesn't love me, she wanted to say. *Like a person who has left me to become less and less.*

"Look, Ter, I'm going to go finish eating dinner now. Have a good time." The line clicked.

Her phone was warm from the effort of finding a signal. She pinned it between her raised knees and pressed hard. She considered pressing until it cracked open between her bones like a shellfish, exposing its meat.

Then Teresa's eye caught movement over by the brush at the edge of the parking lot, the same kind of long dark scurrying twisting shape she'd thought she'd seen the first night. Like a shadow come alive, there and gone so quickly she couldn't be sure of anything. She stood up and stepped closer, pulled by fear and a strange thrill. She wondered what it could be, if it was actually there, what it might feel like against her palms.

"What are you doing, Aunt Terry?"

She whirled. Ellie had just come around the corner of the cabin. Teresa gestured toward the place where the shape had disappeared. "Did you see that?"

"See what? I just see you, looking around..." and here Ellie darted her head back and forth, like a jumpy deer, and giggled.

Teresa couldn't stand that laugh, the license it represented. No one expected kindness out of Ellie. Suddenly this seemed unbearably unfair.

"You know, sometimes I get pretty tired of you," Teresa told her. She said it with relish, though she knew it was the kind of thing someone who should never be a mother would say.

Ellie let out a disbelieving noise. Teresa thought that next her niece would scream, or throw a rock at Teresa's head. But Ellie only turned and ran.

THAT NIGHT TERESA AWOKE AGAIN to the hushed sounds of Granna's departure. "Granna," she said, hoarse with sleep, "where are you going?"

The sounds stopped. For a moment Teresa expected that Granna would return, like a guilty child, to bed.

"I want you to go back to sleep, Teresa," Granna said firmly, and began moving again.

Teresa imagined herself disobeying. She could follow Granna. She could make Granna take her along, out there in the night, where every scrap of darkness might tear itself free of the rest, at any moment, and begin that twisting. It might twist toward them, around them, slipping itself about them like a vine until they were both woven into the blackness, part of it. The imagining became a dream. Teresa went nowhere.

IN THE MORNING GRANNA was back again, and younger. That this was impossible did not make it less true. Teresa watched in disbelief as she spun through their room, getting dressed. She snapped the nightgown she had just removed in the air and folded it crisply, then narrowed her bright eyes and picked at something on the sleeve. She took a little leap toward the dresser to tap a drawer shut. She might have been a sixty-five-year-old who'd just awakened from her most refreshing sleep in a decade.

When Teresa looked up while brushing her teeth and saw the olivey shadows beneath her own eyes, the small fine cracks beginning to spread, she thought, *She is stealing from me.*

It was time to talk to Deb. At the diner after breakfast, Granna stood to visit the bathroom, and Teresa saw her chance. "Ellie, why don't you go play outside?" she asked, once Granna was out of earshot.

"Play outside?" Ellie said. She'd been avoiding Teresa's eyes all morning; now she turned to her mother in outrage.

Deb sighed. "Just wait out front for a minute, honey. There's a bench."

"Great, a bench. My favorite thing, sitting on benches."

"Ellie," Deb said.

Ellie flounced off, stopping on her way out to take a big spiteful helping of mints from the jar on the hostess stand.

Teresa wasted no time—who knew how speedy Granna might be in there? "What do you think about this? About Granna?" she asked Deb.

"It's strange."

"That's all you've got?"

"What do you want me to say, Teresa?"

"She's been getting up in the middle of the night. She must

be going somewhere, doing something." Teresa searched for the right way to explain. "I think somehow she's *making* this happen."

Deb stared.

"We need to figure out how."

Deb shook her head. Her face was settling into the expression that meant she would be difficult to convince. I do not have the energy to worry about this, that face said. Teresa would have been willing to bet that it was, in part, this look—Deb's stiffness when you asked her to stretch—that Deb's husband Jim had walked away from. She wondered what similar bets Deb would have made about her and Adam. "I think you're making too big a deal out of this. Granna's allowed to get up in the night," Deb said.

"That's not the point."

"She's not doing anything wrong. She's getting better." Deb put some money on the table and began to rise. "I really shouldn't leave Ellie out there alone."

TERESA TRIED GRANNA HERSELF later that day, when the two of them fell a little behind the others on their walk; they were taking one of the other trails through the woods. "It's great, Granna, that you're feeling so good," Teresa said.

"Yes."

"Really terrific."

"For me especially," Granna said.

"What do you think it is that's helping? You know, so you can keep it up, once you go back."

"Oh, I'm not sure I'll go back." Granna moved ahead. Beneath the hem of her dress Teresa could see the muscles of Granna's calves cording and releasing, a thick and frightening movement beneath her skin.

WHEN SHE HEARD GRANNA STIRRING that night, Teresa pretended to be asleep. She waited for the sound of the door closing, rose, and slid her feet into her sandals. She took two slow breaths. Then she went out the door herself.

She was only just in time. Disappearing down the path into the woods was a pale, moony, reflected kind of glimmer, like the sheen of a moth's wings—Granna's nightgown. Teresa ran to where it had vanished, and from there she could see it again up ahead of her, floating among the trees.

It was hard to move quietly through the woods at night, though Granna seemed to be managing fine. Teresa tried to tiptoe, tried not to whip branches back and forth. But the ground gave with delicate crunches as she stepped, like some slight-boned thing she was crushing, and twigs poked and caught at her and did their best, in their fragile way, to hold her back. She would not be held back. She wondered how far in Granna was going to take them. Where was it, this place where Granna was doing whatever she was doing to make herself new?

The trees thinned as they approached the swimming hole, so Teresa slowed. She watched as Granna stood at the edge of the water and took off her nightgown—the flesh beneath the same pale, glowing moth-color as the fabric, as if Granna were only shedding one skin to reveal another. Granna entered the water, waded deeper and deeper, and finally gave herself to it. In the center of the swimming hole, where the current slackened, she floated on her back with her face turned to the sky.

Now there were other things moving. The black slinking shape Teresa had been seeing, multiplied: many of them together, moving toward the stream. She blinked, but couldn't quite get a clear look at any single one. *Animal, vegetable, mineral?* her mind recited. Animal, she thought—that low scurrying, that blackness that looked like fur—but they moved too fast and it was too dark to tell for certain. Was she seeing them slip into the stream, swim toward Granna, and circle her, or was that just the movement of the water itself, the play of the moonlight? The water was braiding into a dark mat that seemed to bear Granna up. Granna stretched out her arms as if making a snow angel on the surface, and Teresa swore she saw the shapes brush against her fingertips.

"Teresa!" Granna called.

Teresa stood very still.

"Teresa, I know you're there. I can hear you."

Beneath the trickle of the water, Teresa was sure—almost sure—she heard the slick sounds of moving bodies, and little calls, a squeaking interchange over and through Granna. Lowest of all, clicking noises, like the closing of small sharp teeth.

"Well, you're here." Granna's voice was strong, irritated. "What are you going to do now?"

Yes, what, Teresa wondered?

"If it was the other way around, I wouldn't stop you," Granna said.

Teresa understood that this was true. All those summers, Granna had never stopped her from diving, never even seemed to want to stop her, though her own breath must have caught in her throat while Teresa was underwater. When Teresa resurfaced with her fistfuls of mud and glimmerless stones, Granna had never questioned whether the prizes were worth the cost of their pursuit. She must have needed to breathe deep, slow her heart, but she had never let Teresa see. And when Teresa had lined her stones up on the bank, Granna had guarded them as if they were made of gold while Teresa dove again.

"I won't stop you," Teresa said now.

Granna didn't answer, just swept her arms back and forth. Teresa thought about following her into the water, swimming toward her, sweeping her own arms wide. But she saw that what was happening here didn't belong to her. The gleam of Granna's kicking body, encased in all that dark water—Teresa couldn't take her eyes off it.

After a minute, she made herself turn. She looked for moving shadows as she stumbled back through the woods, though she knew she wouldn't see any. The row of unlit cabins, when she reached it, looked abandoned. She felt a moment's uncertainty about which was hers. Inside, it was very quiet, and cold; Granna had left the window open. Teresa closed it, but the chill remained. She filled a glass with water and drank. A sweater Deb had loaned her hung on the back of the desk chair, and she put it on before she got into bed. She could still see that gleam when she closed her eyes.

Her stomach and arms were cold to the touch. Teresa pressed on them. She lifted the covers and stole a glance beneath, but her skin was too dull to see in the dark. She let the covers fall again and pulled the sweater tighter against herself. The wool was nubby, as if Deb had been picking at it with her nervous fingers.

In the cabin next door, Teresa thought, maybe Deb was lying awake too. She wouldn't be thinking about Teresa, or Granna, or herself. She would be thinking about Ellie, as she probably was most of the time. Ellie who sometimes didn't cross Teresa's mind for days. As she listened to her sleeping daughter's breath, Deb would probably try to match her own breath to that rhythm, hoping to be soothed. And all the while she would be wondering what she always wondered, where Ellie might look, someday, for a hole dark and deep enough to take all of her in and spit her out again, new. Where she might find the right teeth for her skin.

ALL THE KEYS TO ALL THE DOORS

On that first tuesday in march, the assistant principal came to tell Cele what happened. She answered the door still in the thick bathrobe she wore against the achy morning chilliness, still holding her second cup of coffee. His lips were gray around the edges. It was all over; the boy who'd done it was dead. For some reason the doors to the school and the third-grade classroom hadn't been locked. *There will be no more Tuesdays in Middleford*, Cele decided while the assistant principal spoke. She looked over at Kaitlin's dark house and willed her to keep sleeping. *No more month of March either.* She opened her mouth to tell him so.

"What?" she asked. "What did you say?"

MIDDLEFORD WAS A TABLECLOTH of a town, stretched loose and green over gentle New England hills. Anchored by Cele's gifts. Cele gave buildings the way other women gave candies linty from the bottoms of their purses. The town hall, the library, the middle school, the high school, the rec center. Gracious hulks of buildings, Greek temples swathed in brick, monumental. She gave a monument, too, dedicated to the general war dead, which the town festooned with flags on Memorial Day.

These buildings' caretakers were all old men, and Cele hired other old men to replace them when they died. People in town wondered absently how these men, so old, managed to keep the buildings so spotless and clean lined. There was widespread mild worry about their backs. Cele didn't hire them for their backs, but for their discretion. Forty years ago, the first of them had come to talk to her, three months into his tenure at the town hall (the first of her gifts, answering the first, most urgent need, or so she'd then thought— putting the main in Main Street). Sam Brewer, a stooped man of seventy, who took off his hat when he spoke to her. "Something's funny with the building."

"Funny?"

He crossed his arms. He didn't want to say the crazy thing he had come to say. Cele didn't know what it was, though some corner of her had suspected that there'd be something. That faint itching knowledge was what had made her hire Sam for the job in the first place and not some strapping, younger, louder man.

She was quiet. She was only thirty, that long-ago morning, but she'd already learned the power of silence, the way it let you set terms.

Sam finally spoke. "There's no work for me to do. I dust and I mop and I sweep, but it's just to be doing something. There's never dust, or dirt, nothing. Sometimes I'll even see somebody's dropped something, or left a footprint, but when I come back to clean it, it's gone already. Like..."

He let his eyes roam over her living room: The mantel with the blue-and-white Chinese vases her father had set there when he bought this house before Cele was born, with some of the money Cele herself would quadruple. The worn-in chair that had come with Garth when she'd married him. Her father had been dead for ten years, on that morning of Sam's visit, and Garth for two. It was in the aftermath of Garth's death—so unexpected, both of them so young; and so rapid, just months after they'd realized anything was wrong—that Cele had first had the thought to give a building, to try to somehow stick things back in place.

"Like?" Cele prompted Sam, when she couldn't wait anymore.

"Like the building soaks it up."

So it seemed the buildings had gone one step farther than merely assuming the role she'd envisioned for them. They were taking in life and mess as ballast, affixing themselves. Here was some understanding, instead of just that faint itch from before, though the understanding felt like something pulled from her sleeping mind. It made sense to her in the same way her dreams did.

Cele's heart pounded. She raised her eyebrows politely. "I imagine you just don't know your own efficacy, Sam."

In these forty years since, mud, dirt, and dust had continued to vanish, when no one was looking, from the hallways of Cele's buildings. Graffiti continued to disappear from the walls of their bathrooms—the more embarrassing its message, the faster it went. What was more, none of her buildings had ever needed painting, or new roofs, or their brick walls repointed. Cement did not crumble. Furnaces did not break down. Middlefordians assumed Cele had these matters taken care of while they slept. It did not seem beyond her.

Cele herself had never gained a clearer sense of how it worked—what was even working. Mostly, she kept this lack of knowledge a secret from herself.

If only she'd gotten to the elementary school a little earlier. The existing building, which dated from the twenties, was slated for demolition, a new building to be given next year. In one of her buildings, Cele was sure, this could never, ever have happened.

THE ELEMENTARY-SCHOOL assistant principal nearly hyperventilated as he drove them down Main Street, talking rapidly and senselessly. Cele patted her knees and tried to remember his name. John? Jim? The horror of the moment, of course, but even so she couldn't ask. She was seventy now, and she was careful with herself in a way she hadn't bothered with at forty, keeping her gray hair trimmed blunt and precise as the edge of a paintbrush just below her ears, asking only the kinds of questions that betrayed no confusion.

John-Jim was too red where he'd been too pale before. Flooded with blood. Blood-flooded.

"You have to tell them," John-Jim was saying.

Cele blinked. "Who?"

"The families."

"What do you mean?"

"I just told you," he said, though that was a thing people did not say to Cele, people just repeated, if she wanted them to. "Some of the families are at the police station, the ones who can't find their kids, not outside the school, not at the hospital, and no one will tell them anything."

"Well, the police should tell them."

"They will, once they know who exactly, once they've handled..." He blanched again. She willed him not to say it, and knew they were all right when he turned back to red. "The police won't say anything yet, just keep telling them to stay put, and everyone keeps asking and asking, and I don't know what to say to them. I thought you might. You were who I thought of."

Of course she was. Who else? Officially, Cele had no real role in Middleford, was nothing more than a donor, but all Middlefordians knew that titles and actualities were not the same. She'd appeared next to Cal Tompkins at his campaign events, when he was running for First Selectman, and he won in a landslide. Zoning changes, tax increases, plans for new parks required her approval. When Jenny Long, local mother, was dying of ovarian cancer, Cele went to visit her every Thursday, and held a fund-raiser that produced more money than Jenny had been able to use.

But what did John-Jim expect her to say, once he brought her to this room in the police station where the families were gathered? It would be a small room, without enough chairs, she imagined. What could she possibly say, inside it?

Cele's cell phone rang. "Cele, is it true?" Kaitlin's voice, on the line, wavered and caught odd emphases, as if someone were turning the volume on Cele's phone up and down.

"I think so," Cele said, because somehow it seemed kinder than just saying *yes*.

"How can it be? All those kids? All of them?"

Cele pictured Kaitlin hunched over her kitchen table, leaning her rib cage into the wood so the mound of her pregnant stomach could expand beneath. Pressing her palms to that mound, herself and not herself, like a diviner. "Kaitlin, go back to bed," Cele said, firmly enough that maybe she would listen, and hung up. She wanted to imagine Kaitlin snug beneath her quilt.

John-Jim was still talking, maybe had talked right through the phone call. "You have to tell them something. You'll know how to do it."

Crisply, Cele said, "Let me off here, please."

John-Jim pulled to the side of the road with the automatic

obedience that would have returned him to his seat, in school, when instructed. "Here? Why? Please. Please, Mrs. Bailey."

"I have something I need to take care of."

"But—"

She waved a brisk hand and opened the door, a trembling escapee. "Thank you," she said. Shut the door hard, strode away, leaving him no choice, she thought, but to begin driving, though she didn't risk turning her head to see.

The town hall loomed before her. No one would look for her here, not for a while. No one would find her and bring her to those families and make her talk to them. Town offices opened at 9:30 and so the door was still locked, but Cele produced her key chain, choking with all the keys to all her doors, from her handbag.

The air inside had its usual marvelous past-scent, marbly and cured. The quiet was another time's quiet. She breathed it greedily.

Cele knew that Marcia, the town clerk, kept Middleford High School yearbooks in chronological order on a bookshelf in the office on the second floor. *Our kids are the heart of this town,* Marcia said.

A sophomore last year, not enrolled this year, the assistant principal had told Cele. The name was familiar. His parents she could see in her mind, hazy but there: the father was bald and quiet, the mother brown-haired, with a frequent laugh. But she couldn't picture the boy, and his faceless name burrowed and chewed. Not that Cele thought she knew every person in Middleford, but she'd thought she knew the ones who might need various kinds of watching. Not to have known this boy—not to have sensed what was lurking, coiling, readying—was a failing, indicative of larger failings.

Cele took the stairs and opened Marcia's office with another key. There was the yearbook, last in line. Heavy in her hands. She could not open it, but she couldn't leave it either, so she took it with her down the hall to the Meeting

Room, which was Cele's own understanding of Middleford's heart. She came here, sometimes, when she had decisions to make. Forty years ago, it had been the first room she envisioned. The first room of her first building: ceremonial, with a somber lacquer, a place for battle-time strategies. She'd known by then that battles could happen when they were least expected.

She set the yearbook on the rich dark wood table at the center of the room and sat down before it. From the walls, portraits of the town's founders gazed down, peering at the book or at their own reflections in the table's surface. All of Middleford's legends. Where no portrait had existed, and no likeness on which a portrait might be based—many of these people were historically significant only in the most local sense—Cele had commissioned artists to make them up wholesale, so that Middlefordians could have faces to put with the names they knew. Sometimes, when she came in here, she even talked to the founders' portraits. The weight of their gazes helped her hear her own words differently and know what to do.

Cele let herself lay her cheek on the table for a moment. Then she opened the yearbook.

In his picture, the boy looked already dead. Maybe her knowledge was coloring him, but Cele thought he would have looked that way to her yesterday too. The strange pale thinness of the face, as if the flesh were falling away. The eyes canted slightly to the side, looking at what came next. He hadn't been there, not really. Already he'd been beyond touching.

To leave him that way was more than Cele could bear. She pulled a pen from her handbag, detached the cap with a crisp pop, and then her hand became a child-hand and crab-scribbled out the boy's face, plaguing him with a swirling cloud of ink, like a rough rendering of dirt or a swarm of insects.

She dropped the pen. She felt the portraits watching her and looked up.

Such histrionics, said the piggy eyes of Richard Stanley, gentleman apple-farmer, first to call Middleford a town back in 1723, and who had cared enough to argue with him?

Emmeline Lewis, 1940s Middleford schoolteacher, spectacles aglint: *Is it the picture's fault?*

Cele's own father, his jowly, hairless head sculptural, mythic: *You know whose fault it is.*

Garth was last in line, there at all only because Cele had insisted. He gazed at her gently and sadly. *You know.*

A gulping sob ached up Cele's throat and made a soft, low note. She closed the yearbook and shoved it. It zipped across the tabletop that never in this town hall, in this town, would need polishing. She grabbed her keys and shuffled out, slamming the door behind her and locking it. In the bathroom she vomited up her coffee and flushed away the stinging brown.

She quivered, but she felt calmer. The yearbook should be returned to its line. She could do that, at least.

When she opened the door, the book was no longer on the table.

It must have slipped right off the opposite edge. She went to check, though she knew already that it hadn't, because she'd seen it in the middle of the tabletop as she fled. The floor was bare but for the chairs' feet, shaped like lions' paws.

A book, something so large and substantial as a book, she would not have believed. This room, it seemed, could take in a different kind of disarray. Maybe that was what had been happening all those times she'd come here with half-thought-out plans, and said them out loud, and found her thinking suddenly clearer. Or maybe this was a new gift, for today.

She leaned out the Meeting Room door, listening carefully. Nothing stirred. Nothing would stir. The news must have spread by now, and the people who normally reported here to run the sleepy town offices would be at the police station instead, trying to sort out what they were supposed to do.

She stepped back and surveyed the room, asking it a question. The portraits wouldn't meet her eyes.

Then Cele heard stirring, after all. Someone calling "Mrs. Bailey?" and footsteps coming up the stairs. She emerged to find John-Jim panting his way toward her. Cele must have left the front door unlocked. She wasn't the first to forget, today, to lock a door.

"Here you are," he said. "I drove around so you'd have some time. But now you're finished. You are, right? And I can bring you."

Some sickened piece of Cele seemed to have vanished with the yearbook, and she was able to see John-Jim clearly, the whole shaking mess of him. The way a person treading water, breathing deeply, head well clear of the surface, can see every thrash of a distant person as he drowns.

"Are you all right?" she asked.

His face crumpled.

"I saw it," he blurted. "I heard the noise. I went to check what it was. The whole thing, I saw it, through the door."

Cele understood. For the rest of his life, he would know himself to be the person who had seen it happen without somehow stopping it (certainly he couldn't have, but that didn't matter)—just as Cele would know herself to be the person who had not replaced the elementary school in time.

She was able to see, though, whose knowledge was worse.

Behind her, the portraits whispered. The sound gathered texture in her mind. What she did next came from the same sort of instinct that would have led her to cover up a wound— so it could heal, and because it hurt to look at it.

Cele put her hand on the assistant principal's plump elbow. "James," she said, for of course the man's name was James, how could she ever have forgotten? "Come with me."

She showed him to a seat at the table. "Wait here. Just for a minute. I'll be right back."

Cele closed the door behind her, and locked it. James

might or might not have heard the click—it was a quiet lock. She went back to the bathroom and combed her hair into place with her fingers. She looked like herself in the mirror.

When she unlocked and opened the door to the Meeting Room, it was empty, though the chair in which James the assistant principal had been sitting was pushed back from the table just slightly, as if he'd gotten up in a hurry to go wherever he'd gone.

CELE TALKED TO PEOPLE all day long. To the police, to the various reporters who arrived so quickly it seemed they must have scented the event before it actually happened, to members of the school board. To the families. She didn't cry. To cry would be disrespectful—what would it leave for the others to do, with so much more to grieve than she had? Expression had a ceiling whose height must be considered, and where one's claim lay beneath it.

"Where did James go?" said the raw-nosed, weeping elementary-school principal, Heidi Watkins. Heidi had seen nothing. By the time she came out of her office it was all finished.

"I have no idea," Cele told her, not untruthfully.

Cele had Mark Barrows from the police department drive her home, long after dark. Instead of taking the trim path to her own front steps she turned toward Kaitlin's house.

Andrew answered the door. "Oh, thank God," he said, without any of his habitual charming irony. There was a crease down the middle of one of his freckled cheeks, as if he'd been recently in bed. Cele's feelings about Andrew in general were mild, benevolent: he was no worse than anyone would have been. Today she felt grateful he'd been home with Kaitlin all day. She followed him back to where Kaitlin sat, tucked into a corner of the couch, her belly like a pillow she'd positioned herself behind for security, staring at the television.

"They aren't really saying anything new," Kaitlin said. Cele sat down beside her, and Andrew ducked out again.

"They must have already said what they know," Cele told her.

"So what do you know?" Kaitlin turned to face Cele. Always that sharpness to her. It was what made seeing her round in pregnancy so odd—a globe strapped to a collection of angles.

Kaitlin's parents had lived in this house for years, and had begun raising Kaitlin's older brothers and then Kaitlin herself here, before Cele really noticed any of them. Then one Halloween she'd answered a knock at her door to find Kaitlin, who was then about six, in a Dorothy costume on the stoop with her two older brothers, both attired as Star Wars Stormtroopers. Cele had turned fifty that year, and all evening as she'd bestowed candy on neighborhood children, she'd been dogged by a sudden understanding that if these children discussed her after, they would call her *the old woman.*

"You didn't want to be Princess Leia?" she asked Kaitlin.

"I'm Dorothy every year."

"Why?"

"Knowing ahead of time makes everybody feel good."

The two brothers were jostling over Cele's candy-bar selection. Cele peered at the little girl in her wig with its brown braids, a loop of her real, blond hair caught in the band at the forehead.

"What a good thing to have realized," Cele told her.

After that Kaitlin came often to Cele's house to drink juice at the dining room table, dipping her beaky little nose into her cup with each sip and telling Cele about her brothers and teachers and friends and parents. Cele sometimes played a private game while Kaitlin talked, pretending Kaitlin was her child, hers and Garth's. Any child they'd actually had would have been grown by then, of course, but it was just a game.

When Kaitlin went away to college, Cele thought she'd lost her. As it turned out, Kaitlin had only found Andrew and brought him back here, where she took a job teaching fifth grade at Middleford Elementary. "Middleford just feels more real than other places," she'd told Cele.

"Yes," Cele had said, thinking of all the bricks she'd piled. But Kaitlin had never shown any sign of suspecting the bricks' role. To her, it seemed, Middleford's stability was simply one of its features, like the sharp curve on Main Street, or the tea-colored, leaf-clogged pond at the north edge of town.

Once Kaitlin began spending her days at the elementary school, Cele had wanted to bump up its replacing in her plans. But the original building was still sound enough, and the foundation of the middle school had cracked. To switch the order would have been to make an admission of something.

Now, Cele held Kaitlin's bony, oddly warm hand. "Well, what have they been saying?" she said, and Kaitlin began to recite the numbers and the names and the sequence of locations—parking lot to front door to classroom, and why weren't the doors locked? That question again.

"That's all I know too," Cele told her. "Nobody knows more than that now."

"You must." Kaitlin's nose ran. She rubbed it angrily.

"It was third grade, Kaitlin. It was far away from your wing," Cele said.

"I know that."

If Cele knew what Kaitlin wanted to hear, she'd say it. She was used to understanding Kaitlin, but since Kaitlin's pregnancy and especially since her maternity leave had begun two weeks earlier, Kaitlin had been saying things Cele couldn't see to the bottom of. *I wish there were a window in my stomach, so I could look at all his parts and organs and everything and make sure it's all in the right place,* she said, making Cele think of cadavers hacked up by medical school students. *I wish I knew every thought my son was ever going to have.* Cele had never felt that way about another person, not even Garth, whom she'd loved until she felt she was about to split open.

I think having a child is the most terrifying thing a person can ever do to themselves.

"What else do you want to know?" Cele asked.

"I want to know *why*. I want to know what was wrong with him, that he did this. What his reasons were."

"The reasons of people like this aren't reasons. They don't help anything."

"It would help me, to know."

Cele said what would help Kaitlin was going to bed. Bundled her up the stairs. Andrew appeared and watched from the top, and Cele felt better, knowing that Kaitlin only had to traverse the staircase itself alone. Halfway, Kaitlin stopped and turned back.

"Cele," she asked, "what are those mothers going to do?"

CELE SAT IN HER BEDROOM that night and held her keys in her lap. She hadn't been able to leave them downstairs. The weight of them, in the dip between her thighs, pulled the material of her nightgown tight, like somebody's sleeping hand. Two of the rings held all the keys they could; the last was almost full. If that last ring had been a clock face, the keys took up all the room between ten and two. The key to every door in every building Cele had built was on one of these three rings. Nothing special, in itself, this key chain— just a cracked black plastic fob and the large metal rings— other than the fact that it had been Garth's, once.

Because the elementary school wasn't hers yet, Cele had no keys to it. So she couldn't touch the ones for the front door, the third-grade classroom, and wonder why their corresponding locks had not been thrown that morning. Probably there was no real reason, only that locking them had never been necessary before. Probably it wouldn't have mattered anyway.

Cele had visited the elementary school along with the other schools this winter, as she did every year. There was no official justification for these visits, of course, but no one was going to tell her she couldn't. She went because she wanted to watch the children's faces at the middle school and the high school, looking for signs that they could feel the buildings' hunger for the gum they stuck under their desks, the crumpled paper that fell short of trash cans, the clumsier of their words. At the elementary school, she laid plans for new classroom spaces as she sat against back walls and listened to lessons. She stayed no longer in Kaitlin's classroom than in any of the others, just as she'd promised herself ahead of time. But she loved watching Kaitlin at the front of the room, her belly then just visibly swelling, teaching a lesson on *The Witch of Blackbird Pond*. It seemed exactly the right place, in all the world, for Kaitlin to be.

The elementary-school children, too, had demanded Cele's attention. They twitched with their wants and fears. Chewing on pencils and fingers, sucking on swatches of their own hair, as if they were trying to take their world inside themselves.

Cele counted her keys now, for the soothingness of it, the way a miser counts coins. Eighty-two. Each key attached to a space she could open at will. Locks mattered. Locks made you owner. Plus there was all they let you keep in, and out.

Cele wasn't sure what that meant for James. She had no guesses about where he was now, if he was anywhere. What she'd done was horrible, maybe, except it didn't feel that way. If she'd known what would happen when she locked him in the Meeting Room, she was almost sure she wouldn't have been brave enough, though it was true she had never been lacking in bravery. Really, she was sure of nothing except what she'd relieved him of, what his life in Middleford would have been like after this day. She had no means of evaluating the rightness or wrongness of closing that door, turning that lock, but at least it was a decision, a shaping. Better, perhaps, than the formlessness of accident—a forgotten lock, or two, the imbalances of one boy, a rogue and energetic cell in the bloodstream—reverberating and knocking things down.

The new elementary school would come with maybe twenty-five keys, all told. Cele closed her eyes, pinched the pads of her fingers together, and imagined those keys between them, each jagged tooth. But she couldn't seem to give them the weight of metal in her mind. They stayed light as toothpicks, light as fingernails, light as hair.

THE REPORTERS SETTLED IN and got comfortable. Their stories in print and on television made Cele ill—they used quaint postcard-like pictures of Middleford that they'd tinted gray, and horror-movie music hummed in all their prose. To discover more about THE YOUNG MAN they talked to his three-doors-down neighbor, and trumpet teacher, and dentist, and former classmate. Watery collages of details about the children and their teacher were assembled. Cele unplugged her television and threw away her newspapers still in their bags.

Schools stayed closed, all that week and into the next. The streets were empty of Middlefordians but chock-full of rubberneckers from near and far. On her way to buy groceries, Cele was tempted to run down with her car a pair of middle-aged women, pointing and clutching each other on the street, cheeks rouged by titillation.

Garth had always told Cele she was ruthless. He said it with warmth but also with wonder. Somehow he'd spied this sort of impulse in her, even then.

James's family seemed only a little concerned about where

he had gone. Cele took this impossibility for a reassuring sign, a demonstration of rightness, like the failure of anyone in town to ever demand an explanation for her buildings' strange self-repair. James's wife told somebody James must be *clearing his head,* and that was the explanation that circulated. The question of his current location seemed papered over: there, and everyone knew it, but nobody looked at it. He'd become part of the anchoring, maybe, Cele thought, which they all needed more than ever. Part of what the buildings sucked in to keep this town in place.

Meanwhile, Kaitlin stopped brushing her hair, allowing it to become a pale knotty cloud. She wore the same black sweatpants and T-shirt every day and began to take on the smell of overripe fruit. Andrew had gone back to work, and Cele thought it might have been better in some ways if Kaitlin could have returned to teaching; the children would have asked questions, and made mistakes, and dropped things, and stopped seeming like symbols of anything. But of course the school wasn't even open. Cele adopted the routine she'd imagined for a month from now, after the baby was born, having Chinese food delivered to Kaitlin and Andrew's, or stopping by to make coffee. Their house seemed so quiet, quieter somehow than Cele's own.

"Cele, what do you remember about Sonya Cummings?" Kaitlin asked, one rainy Thursday.

"You worked down the hall from her. You don't need me to remember her for you."

"When she was a kid, I meant."

Cele considered. In her mind, she stripped Sonya's face of its middle-aged fleshiness. "She was noisy. That's probably not surprising. She loved jump rope, I think."

Kaitlin chewed on her lips. "She always sounded like she was reading Hallmark cards. I keep trying to imagine what she'd have said about this."

"There isn't a card for this," Cele said.

Kaitlin waddled to the sink and banged her tea mug down inside, hard enough to rattle the spoon. "Jump rope? I can't picture that at all."

"Well, she was smaller then."

When Kaitlin turned around, she'd lifted the spoon from the cup, and she brandished it at Cele. "I don't think," she said, "I want this baby to be born."

"Of course you do," Cele said briskly. But she was seeing her buildings bulging, their seams stretching, thinking how it would be if everything they'd kept safe and hidden inside were about to burst forth. Her knees trembled.

Kaitlin threw the spoon. It sounded much larger than it was, hitting the floor.

"Cele, why didn't you build a new elementary school?" she said, and Cele was surprised enough that she had to sit down. Kaitlin sat, too. She watched Cele, who had no answer for her.

After a moment, Cele stood and picked up the thrown spoon. She washed it carefully, running her thumb along its rim. Dried it and put it silently back in its drawer.

THE NEXT DAY, Cele decided on gardening. She would plant hardy early-spring flowers so Kaitlin could see some color when she looked out the window. If she seemed to notice, Cele would plant some at her house too.

Cele's legs didn't like folding up so she could kneel on the ground—when had that happened, that they'd stopped listening to her without complaint?—but her fingers bent easily, dug easily. She enjoyed the feel of the soil. Cool and moist, like touching the deepest dark. She made holes for the pink and purple pansies and wondered about herself, whether her legs or her fingers foretold her future. Part of her was still sure she would turn out to be like her buildings. In two hundred years she would still be a fixture, and no one would quite know how old she was, and new Middlefordians would still be allowing her to stow them away in safe compartments. The prospect made her tired.

Astonishing, that Kaitlin should know about the buildings. Maybe the knowledge had just then risen up from Kaitlin's depths like a bubble. Or maybe she'd known all along and never said a word.

The first pansy Cele planted settled perfectly straight. She tucked a mound of dirt around the roots, patted it firm.

When she turned to reach for the next, she found that the mothers were coming up her walkway.

A pack of them. A tribe of grief. Ella McIntyre, who'd cried loudest of any at the police station, led the way. They stopped, their toes at the edge of the flat of pansies.

"What can you do for us?" Ella said to Cele.

"I'm sorry?"

"What can you *do*?" the blond Perkins mother said. Cele had never known her first name.

Why the mothers had come this way, all together, Cele had no idea. Perhaps the fathers would come up her path tomorrow, or next month, and then the grandmothers, and the grandfathers, and the siblings.

But the mothers were here now, waiting for their answer. Cele could tell them there was nothing. They'd have to believe her. *Who do you think I am?* she could say.

The mothers had white, nervous fingers. They had dry, blasted eyes. Their feet shuffled in place. From some things, Cele thought, there was no recovering. She should know— Garth's death had been that, almost, for her. To turn it into only *almost*, to give herself enough heft to keep from floating away, she'd had to weigh down all of Middleford. There wasn't enough space on the whole surface of the earth to build what it would take to reaffix these mothers. Their pain was a vast, unchartable, unimaginable sea. Cele couldn't see its edges. She wasn't sure it had any, but if it did, they were beyond the reach of her mind, and beyond the reach of the mothers' minds too.

Well, what, then? People lived with unlivable things all the time. There was no rule that Cele had to watch them try.

Cele looked up at them, right into all those faces. Rules, though, had never had much to do with the actual shape of Cele's life. These women weren't Cele's responsibility, except that she'd decided long ago they all were.

"Come with me," Cele told them.

She led the silent line of mothers to the town hall. She could feel them behind her, like a black held breath. They were suspended, all of them, in the same moment, though it would look different to each. An orange backpack, a crooked braid, new nail polish, a tooth lost the night before. The way their treasure had looked the last time they'd seen it. None of these women was ever getting out of this moment, and it was too much to expect them to drag it around with them through the rest of their slow, slow lives. Cele felt sure that whatever she was bringing them to must be better than that. She imagined it as a long white room full of narrow beds with crisp sheets. They would each get in, and lay the blackness down, and rest their eyes on a white ceiling.

The Meeting Room seemed to sigh as the mothers entered. They took their places around the table. They planted their elbows on the wood, leaned their heads into their hands. Some of them closed their eyes.

"Just a moment. I'll be right back," Cele told them. She closed and locked the door.

ONE OF THE FATHERS was interviewed on television, a few days later. Cele, who'd plugged her TV in again, watched him speak. "I think she just went off somewhere," the father said. "I think she needed to."

The mothers had gone off. James was clearing his head. The caretakers Cele hired were unusually strong and efficient men, especially given their age. Vast soundless hands placed new roofs, when needed, in the middle of the night. These stories were Cele's gift to Middleford; something, if not as much as she would have liked.

Cele jingled her keys. She carried them everywhere with her now.

WHEN CELE BROUGHT over a pizza the following week, Andrew met her at the door. He tugged Cele into the coat closet. "She isn't getting better," he said. "Everybody else is getting better."

If Garth had been able to see what happened to Cele after he died, he would not have thought her ruthless. She stopped getting out of bed. It had soothed her to fold the blanket in a certain fashion: lying down, she would make a pleat at the top edge, then double it over, again, again, until it was thigh-level and she would have had to sit up to keep folding. Then she unfolded, up and up, tucking herself back in. Then she started over. She spent whole days doing that. In a different version of her life, she might have spent whole years. Garth would have been terrified, watching her drift, and he would have tried and tried to throw her lines. She was grateful she hadn't ever had to see Garth look the way Andrew looked just now.

Eventually, Cele swam back in. She couldn't quite remember why, or how. One day she got up instead of staying in bed, and the rest followed. This time she just had to tow Kaitlin with her, that was all. Kaitlin was not like the mothers, or James—she could not be that far out. There was no reason for her to be that far. Cele would bring her back in.

Cele put a hand on Andrew's shoulder and used a muted

version of her bullhorn voice, the one from her ribbon-cutting ceremonies. "Kaitlin will be fine, Andrew."

"I hope so," Andrew said.

After Kaitlin had eaten a piece of the pizza, Cele draped her in a sweater and brought her to see the pansies. The cardigan hung like open curtains, unable to button over Kaitlin's stomach.

The flowers were taking, and they nodded their cheerful heads. Kaitlin stooped as if to smell them. Then she began ripping them up.

When she'd finished, when all the pansies lay limp on the grass, Kaitlin said to Cele, "Please."

"Please what? What do you want me to do?" Cele asked. "Just tell me."

"Wherever you took the others," Kaitlin said. "Take me."

Cele was willing to swim with Kaitlin forever, pull and pull, but she hadn't thought to ask Kaitlin if the pulling hurt. Because it wasn't just Kaitlin, after all. Kaitlin had to pull somebody else with her. Extra drag. Cele hadn't thought of that. How could she have? How could she know what that felt like?

"I'll just show you," Cele said. "I'll show you and you can decide."

Cele drove Kaitlin to the town hall. It was too far for Kaitlin to walk, now that she was so big. Carefully, she shepherded Kaitlin toward the Meeting Room, hand on Kaitlin's shoulder as she climbed the stairs. They stood together outside the door while Cele grabbed for the keys in her purse, fumbled them, grabbed again.

"Easy," she said, mostly to herself.

"Easy peasy," Kaitlin said absently.

Cele turned. Kaitlin held the small of her own back, eagerly watching the door, as if behind it were nectar or balm. Cele didn't think that was wrong, exactly. Still, there was Kaitlin's face, the precious warm fact of it. She touched Kaitlin's smooth cheek, and Kaitlin's eyes darted to Cele's face, then back to the door again.

She would only be giving Kaitlin a choice, but she didn't want Kaitlin to have this choice. Did not want the possibility of having to close this door on her, having to stand outside and fit the key to the lock and turn. Why should Cele have to be the one to do it, over and over again?

Cele asked Kaitlin to sit on the stairs. "There's something I need to check inside," she said.

Kaitlin sat down, off-balance, front-heavy.

"Be careful," Cele told her.

Cele went in and closed the door. She twisted the lock so Kaitlin wouldn't come in. She thought about whoever had been the last person into the elementary school that morning, and of Sonya Cummings inside her third-grade classroom, both of them closing doors and stopping short of this one last movement.

Cele walked to the head of the table and set down her keys. She kept her eyes on the shine of them against the wood and tried to make her voice as strong as it had been when she'd come into this room to talk over other decisions, over the years, back when she had thought she was talking only to herself. "I don't want these. I don't want to do it anymore," she said. She felt so light without the keys in her hand.

That isn't all you've brought us.

She looked up. At the end of the row, beside Garth, was the yearbook photo of the boy with his scribbled-out face. Large as the others, framed like the others. Through the ink she could still make out his features.

"Not you," she said.

Garth's eyes sparkled. All their eyes sparkled. Wet, deep as small seas, then not small, widening. Cele looked back at the door, the lock on the door, which she herself had thrown.

THE SALTWATER CURE

THE LODGERS AT PILGRIM'S INN were a parade of walking wounded. When they stood at the front desk and asked Rob for the keys to their rooms, their afflictions made it impossible for them to meet his eyes. Growths and abscesses, limps and stutters, palsies like private earthquakes. Furious rashes and rickety gaits. All of them come for the salt marsh out of which Rob's mother had promised miracles.

Not everyone's wounds could be so clearly seen, though, for the world, in 1932, was finding new ways to injure. Some of the guests were men who came to the inn wearing the suits they had worn to their last days of work; some were women with moth-eaten dresses and moneyed voices who called Rob "boy." Sound enough of body but broken still, and hoping, like the others, that here they might find cures.

When Rob first saw Anne-Marie, he could see no sign of wounds at all, even subtle ones. The morning of her arrival was hot and slow. Rob usually spent his man-the-desk time reading adventure stories, but that June he found he didn't feel the same about them. He wouldn't be returning to school in the fall—he was sixteen now, and his mother thought it time to stop paying others for the jobs he could do during school hours—and he was beginning to suspect that these books about heroic men doing heroic things mocked him. He was growing in strange ways, his arms suddenly too long for the rest of him, his feet too large. His ears also stuck out too far—this had always been the case, but now he knew it. There was a new sort of buzzing in his joints that made it difficult to sit still, yet once he'd finished his chores, he had nowhere to go. So he sat, sharpened his pocketknife, and tried not to imagine sitting in this same chair all summer and fall. Five years from now, or ten.

On the wall beside the front desk hung a framed newspaper article about Betsy Foster, patron child-saint of Pilgrim's Inn, with a small accompanying photograph. That morning Rob watched it with resentment, as if it owed him an explanation. The man in Room 6 called down for more towels. An old woman tottered to the desk to check in to the room reserved under Carlson. Rob had to lean forward to hear her, and then he could smell her: dark rooms and thick blankets, dusty wool and old, yellowed lace. She dropped her key twice on her way to the staircase. He was listening for the thumps of her body falling down the stairs, ready to run and maybe somehow catch her, when Anne-Marie appeared.

She stood in the doorway with her head turned to one side. Something in the yard must have caught her attention. Her hair was red, and her slippery-looking dress matched its shade exactly. A deep wine color that Rob could almost taste between his teeth.

Then she turned her face forward. As she neared the desk,

he saw that she was not quite the girl he'd first taken her for. A few threadlike lines rayed the corners of her eyes, and there was a gold band on her finger. She leaned her elbows on the counter, and suddenly he could smell her too: water and light, as if she'd just sprung fresh from some depth into the air.

But why are you here? he wanted to ask her. What could be wrong with you?

"You can't see the ocean from the door," she said. "The advertisement lied."

Rob's mother had written PILGRIM'S INN: WATCH THE WAVES FROM OUR FRONT DOOR, BATHE IN OUR SALT MARSH, AND EXPERIENCE HEALING, BODY AND SOUL.

"If you stand on a chair you can."

"Do your guests often stand on chairs?"

The door to the back office banged. Rob's mother emerged, bearing a fresh stack of the "health-promoting aromatic sachets" (nine-tenths sawdust) that they gave to the guests upon check-in, along with a brochure of health tips. She set them on the counter and lit up her business smile, all gentle eyes, for the red-haired woman. "Welcome to Pilgrim's Inn. I'm Sarah Simmons. I see you've met my son, Rob."

"Anne-Marie Duncan."

The name fell on Rob's ears and caught, reverberating softly, like the sound of the sea in a shell.

"Your room is all ready for you, Mrs. Duncan. There's time for the salt marsh before dinner, if you'd like."

Anne-Marie's red eyebrows arched, and her eyes flicked to Betsy's article on the wall, then back to Rob's mother's face. Rob felt suddenly sure that Anne-Marie had come here to undo everything. He was surprised by his own eagerness to see what everything would look like, undone.

But all Anne-Marie said was, "Thank you." She took her aromatic sachet and her room key—9—and disappeared up the stairs.

"Well, get back to work, then," Rob's mother told him,

though there wasn't a thing that needed doing. Before she returned to her office, she gave him the sigh of a fellow weary soldier.

THE INSPIRATION FOR THE INN had come to Rob's mother through the newspaper, which she liked to say was the source of all her best ideas. Usually she meant the clothing advertisements. Nobody could make cheap clothes that looked like expensive clothes the way Rob's mother could; she chose fabrics whose colors distracted from their shoddiness, and she sewed fast, just well enough that her customers were some miles or days away from her shop by the time the weakness of the seams became apparent. But that morning three years ago, her message had awaited her on the very front page: PLYMOUTH GIRL RECOVERS. A year into the Depression, the *Plymouth Tribune* assumed its readers were hungry for any crumb of good news they could get. "Hmm," Rob's mother had said. She read the article aloud to him while he chewed on toast. Betsy Foster, local twelve-year-old, had bathed in a salt marsh just outside of town and experienced what her parents described as a near-total remission of her polio symptoms.

Rob's mother turned to the classifieds.

The next day they found a ride across town and negotiated the purchase of the bankrupt cranberry farm of one Mr. Elkinson—twenty acres that included, in addition to the freshwater farm, a salt marsh. "That girl went swimming here?" Rob asked his mother.

"Close enough," she said.

Mr. Elkinson met with them himself. He showed them around the land, walking rapidly, as if they were pursuers he hoped to shake off. Boards were coming loose on the side of his barn, hanging at deranged angles. He caught Rob staring at the bare place beneath, and Rob, ashamed, looked away.

Two months later they held a going-out-of-business sale at the clothing shop and moved into Mr. Elkinson's old farmhouse, its surfaces spruced up with some carpentry work and paint. The barn had been torn down. Rob didn't quite know where the money for these improvements had come from, but this was only the latest flowering of the same talent that had kept him fed and clothed his whole life. His mother had handpainted a sign to hang above the front porch: PILGRIM'S INN.

"Because of the Pilgrims and all, but also because coming here will *feel* like making a pilgrimage. See? We'll make sure it does," she said.

Rob thought about the original Pilgrims, who'd borne their high black hats and their stripped-down lives across a whole ocean and landed on a patch of shore not too far from here—how they would have hated sharing a name with the kind of faith his mother was banking on. She had a way of rewriting things so they read as she wanted them to.

They had been ministering to their pilgrims ever since.

ROB DIDN'T KNOW if Anne-Marie Duncan would take his mother's suggestion and go down to the salt marsh to bathe, but his head was too full of images he hadn't seen yet (her uncovered skin in the open air, the way a drenched suit might cling to her) to leave him any choice but to go, just in case. As soon as check-in hours had passed, he took off his shoes, rummaged in the garden shed until he found a rake, and carried it to the inn's beach.

Calling it a beach was generous. There was no sand, only dune grass that thinned as it neared the shoreline so that the peat showed through like a balding man's scalp. Near the high-tide mark was a line of whitewashed chaise lounges, where their guests often sat to stare at the water and breathe in the mud's rich sulfur smell while they steeled themselves for submersion. This mud was never quite dry.

The sun-warmed wet that seeped between Rob's toes as he approached had the temperature of something living. He could see even from a distance that Anne-Marie was not by the white chairs and not in the water, either. The only people here were the man from Room 7 and his spindly, pale son. The man stood waist deep in the water with the boy belly down on the surface before him. Each time the boy started to sink, his father would lift him, then take his hands away and say hopelessly, "Kick, Thomas, kick!" before surrendering and lifting him again. Rob wanted to tell them to stop, that it would be easier on both of them.

She could still come, Rob figured. He began to rake at the patch of peat just behind the chaise lounges, pulling the sparse grass long and flat.

He had gathered a small pile of dry strands and driftwood by the time the man from Room 7 emerged from the water, wrapped his son in a towel, and slung him over one shoulder for the walk back up to the inn. "Oh, hello," Rob heard the man say to someone, but he kept his own eyes on the ground.

"And hello to you," said the answering voice. Rob let himself look: Anne-Marie in a tomato-colored suit, setting her towel down on one of the chaise lounges while the man and his son passed her. With her hair in a bathing cap, she looked somehow ceremonial. Her skin was so white there was a slight haze around her bared neck and arms and legs in the sunlight. She put her hands to her hips. Shame usually bowed their other guests, propelling them from the safe station of the chaise lounges to the water, from one hiding place to another, but none of that seemed to touch her. Rob felt almost angry. This is a place for sick people, he thought. She isn't sick.

He stopped raking. "Is everything you own red?"

Though she hadn't looked in his direction before, she didn't seem startled by his voice. "I do like red."

She stepped into the water while he eyed the slim shape of

her from behind. Across her shoulders was a light sand-colored stain of freckles, visible only the way a watermark on paper is visible; he wasn't sure he would have been able to make it out in a different light. She extended her hands atop the water, palms down, as if touching a solid surface, and stood that way for a moment. Then she plunged them beneath and went through the same motions that all the bathing guests performed to get themselves ready to swim, scooping water up, patting it along her upper arms. All this though the marsh, stagnant and shallow, was never really cold. Its warmth and brackishness, its heavy animal smell, all seemed to promise that any swimmer would emerge teeming with moist life—yet Rob had always found that the salt actually dried and stiffened his skin, so that his knuckles and knees had a slight leathery crackle when he was back on land again.

"Can't be that cold," he called.

"Oh, all right." She dove.

A lonely silence fell while she streaked forward. But when she surfaced again, she faced the shore.

"So, Rob, is it just you and your mother here? Or is there a Mr. Simmons?"

"He died in the war."

So his mother had always told him. Rob had ceased to believe her years ago when he'd noticed the way his father shape-shifted in her descriptions. The man took on whatever defining traits she found it convenient to emphasize at the moment: when Rob wouldn't eat his carrots, his father turned out to have had a healthy universal appetite, and when Rob left streaks on the windows he had cleaned, his father's diligence had been remarked upon by all who knew him. The war-death was useful in making the case for bravery when Rob, waking from nightmares, had called out for her. Most of Rob's mother's illusions worked best over short periods of time. Still, there was something in the story about his father's death—its finality, maybe—that seemed true as well as useful to Rob, and so he told it, even now, whenever someone asked.

"That's sad," Anne-Marie said, but Rob could tell her heart wasn't in it. She turned and paddled a little distance, not out but to the right. Rob remembered to rake again.

When she stopped swimming, he asked, "What brings you here?" This question went against the rules of Pilgrim's Inn: you did not ask about or otherwise refer to the guests' ailments, even if they were staring you in the face with blood-rimmed eyes. But Anne-Marie had asked about his father. He figured he could ask her this.

"Just passing through, on my way down to the Cape."

That was when Rob believed, for the first time, that something might be wrong with her after all. The studied lightness of her voice, and the notion that Pilgrim's Inn could be on the way to anywhere.

Anne-Marie kept talking, kicking her feet. "My husband's old roommate from school has a place down there, right on the ocean. So perfect it's in bad taste almost, like a children's postcard. You know, seashell cutouts on the shutters. The Cape is nice, though. You can bake yourself half to death."

"I've been." He felt angry again, stupidly, that she'd mentioned her husband, and that she spoke of the Cape as if he would never have seen it. He and his mother had stayed in a cottage in Bourne once with a friend of hers, a big-shouldered man whose name he couldn't remember now.

Anne-Marie fluttered her fingers in the water. "Not that the Cape has *real* beaches. South America has those. Everything bigger, and palm trees everywhere."

"You've been to South America?" A brightly colored image seized him—blue, enormous waves—but he blinked it away before it could give him the same feeling the adventures in his books did.

"My husband is a journalist. We've traveled all over."

Your husband didn't travel here, Rob thought.

"Listen, would you bring me that towel?" she asked.

He dropped the rake, shook her towel out in the air, and carried it to the water's edge. When she walked ashore, she didn't reach for it but turned her back. His heart sped. At the base of her neck, a single red lock had escaped her cap, fatly saturated, stretching down her back like a line of paint over those translucent freckles. Rob wanted to press his lips there. He began to fold the towel around her, and she raised her hands to take it from him just inches from her own shoulders. Had she let him finish the wrapping—and he thought, he thought she almost had—she would have been encircled in his arms.

ROB'S MOTHER MET HIM on his way up from the beach twenty minutes later. He'd stared at the water for a while after Anne-Marie left. "Where have you been?" his mother asked. She pursed her lips at the rake in his hand. "I told you this morning—we'll need more tea before dinner."

He leaned the rake against the side of the house and followed his mother around the front desk, where she handed him the tin of Lipton's and their own tin with PILGRIM'S INN inscribed on the cover. They would pass this second tin around to the guests, after the meal, for a small additional charge that would appear on their final bills. "Take it onto the back porch. I've been drying the mint there. Crumble it nice and fine, and put plenty in—tea doesn't grow on trees."

"All right." Rob paused. "That woman who checked in today," he said, his voice as light as Anne-Marie's. "What do you think is wrong with her?"

"It could be any number of things. Pick some more mint when you're done, and start it drying." She straightened her white apron. In the time that they had been running Pilgrim's Inn, Rob's mother was coming to look more and more like a nurse.

"Don't you think you should know? If you're taking her money?"

She stopped and looked at him, surprised. Rob was surprised, too—he couldn't recall ever saying such a thing to his mother before. Anne-Marie seemed to have somehow summoned these words from him.

"No," his mother said. "I don't need to know. I know we'll help her, that's what matters. Anyway, do you want to eat or don't you?"

The man from Room 7 appeared at the bottom of the stairs, without his son. "Mr. Holbrook!" Rob's mother said. "Is Thomas taking a rest? Working on his appetite for dinner, I hope."

"Yes, exactly." Mr. Holbrook walked toward them, smoothing his hair. He was about Rob's mother's age, though he looked more drawn, more tired than she did; Rob's mother did not allow the world to catch her feeling tired. Rob noticed that the skin around Mr. Holbrook's lips was a little raw, like he'd been licking at them. "He seems better today," Mr. Holbrook said.

"Oh, good."

"I think those calisthenics worked wonders, truly."

Rob had seen part of calisthenics this morning while he mopped pollen off the front porch, and he remembered Thomas slumped and winded. Rob's mother ran the classes herself. They'd involved some actual exertion, like jogging in place, until, a few months in, a man had fainted. Now she just asked everyone to raise their arms in the air and hold them, and stand first on one foot and then on the other "for rebalancing." She and Mr. Holbrook smiled now with a falseness that each must have seen on the other's face. A current of this pretense ran through many conversations at Pilgrim's Inn, which Rob had always accepted without thinking about it much. All at once, he had an urge to step out from behind the desk and take gray-faced Thomas by one hand and the tea tin in the other. He would make Mr. Holbrook crumble the mint for his son's useless tea himself, make his mother feel Thomas's bony arms. Make them face things as they were. What were they all doing here, he wondered?

"I mean," Mr. Holbrook said, "I guess I hoped the improvement would be more *dramatic*. But still, it's there. Steps in the right direction."

Rob's mother drew her eyebrows together. "This is your third day with us, isn't it? Tell me, how many times has Thomas been in the marsh?"

"Three. Once each day."

"Yes, it's often after the third time that we start to see these slow signs of improvement, the sort of thing you mentioned." Though Mr. Holbrook had mentioned nothing but "wonders" and "steps." She pointed with her chin to Betsy Foster's picture frame. "You know," she said, lowering her voice, "this detail wasn't in the papers, but it wasn't until after her *seventh* swim that Betsy's gait really began to even."

"Well, I don't think Thomas is up for swimming more than once a day. He gets tired, you know. And we're leaving tomorrow." He paused. "The seventh swim, you said." A new eagerness was coming into Mr. Holbrook's face.

"That's right," Rob's mother said, and then she waited.

"Perhaps we should extend our stay, just by a day or two? Do you think?" Mr. Holbrook said.

"Oh, very wise," she told him.

ROB WATCHED ANNE-MARIE all through dinner, though he tried not to let her see him doing it. She sat by herself, a few tables away from Rob and his mother, in a yellow dress, with her hair gathered at the nape of her neck. When she dropped her fork and it made a small clunk against the tabletop, Rob flinched, and he thought Anne-Marie smiled. Mr. Holbrook, at the next table, turned and said something to her that Rob couldn't hear. She laughed politely.

Nothing red on her this time, Rob thought, but then she swiveled in her chair so that her feet were facing him, almost as if she were signaling, and recrossed her legs. Red high-heeled shoes. He saw them and a jolt went straight to his groin.

Rushing to his room after dinner to be alone with the idea of her, Rob almost collided with Anne-Marie in the flesh. "Good Lord," she said. She flattened herself dramatically against the wall, and he was sure she thrust her chest just a bit toward him. "*Please*, go ahead. You must have places to be."

He searched for some clever response.

She smiled. "Fine, then," she said, and passed him, her red shoes marking time, heel-toe, heel-toe against the wood floor.

Rob threw the blankets and even the sheets off his bed that night. He lay still on his back, trying to bear his longing. If he could just tell what was wrong with her, he thought, that would help somehow, would even things out between them. He would search for clues—he would run his mind over her, every inch of her that he had seen.

He started with her feet. Did she move them strangely? Did walking seem to hurt her? But he could not think of them without thinking of the red shoes. On from the feet, then. He ascended just to her ankles and saw them flashing through the water as she kicked loosely to keep herself afloat. Her calves, her knees, up, up to the red suit and all that it covered, how she had dripped when she emerged from the water, the cool of her as she'd stood before him and waited for her towel—a bit of anticipation in the angle of her neck, as if she knew what he wanted to do, as if she were also considering it—a cool he could feel in the air coming off her as he almost, almost touched her wet skin. Under his fingertips what a new world it would have been, what rich slipping.

After he had attended to himself there in the dark, he rolled over onto his side. He thought briefly of Pauline Somers, a girl from school with two thick plaits of blond hair. He'd loved Pauline for most of the past year, though she had eyes only for Roger Brooks, and when she gazed at Roger, those eyes went flat and foolish in a way that had been hard to overlook. Still, he'd spent time imagining her as the impetus for great deeds, epic quests. There had also been Missy Sherman, who'd come with him to the church carnival in May and whom he'd bought cotton candy and then kissed on a bench at the end of the night, liking her warmth, the curve of her waist under his palms, the sticky sour-sweet of her mouth.

Missy had told him she couldn't go to the movies with him after all, once she learned he was done with school. "I'm not going away or anything. It's just my mother needs me," he'd protested.

"Yes, your *mother*," she'd said, as if she knew something about Rob's mother that he himself didn't.

Now Pauline and Missy both seemed indistinct, muffled in ordinariness. Gazing into the dim glow of the sky outside his window, Rob couldn't picture either of their faces.

IN THE MORNING, while Rob's mother believed he was sweeping the upstairs hallway, he let himself into Anne-Marie's room and shut the door behind him. He went into guests' rooms all the time to clean; he very well might have been cleaning now. Anne-Marie had driven into the center of Plymouth with some other guests, on some errand or other, and he would hear the car's approach if they returned early. From his desk, Rob had watched her leave and seen the key to Room 9 dangling there on its hook. He'd known he would not be able to resist, so he hadn't made much of an effort.

He stood in the center of the room for a moment.

Somewhere in here was the information he needed about Anne-Marie's sickness, of mind or of body. Somehow he was sure that his not knowing had hung in the air between them and stopped him from touching her. She'd been within reach by the marsh and again in the hall, and there had never been a thing he wanted more than he wanted his hands on her, his mouth on her, the feel of her everywhere on him. Knowing would be a kind of touch; once he knew, other things might be possible. Maybe he could make her see that his knowing made her less alone—that he would fight whatever it was, that no husband who would let her come to Pilgrim's Inn by herself could have taken on this battle as Rob would. He let himself imagine this, how he could go with her, wherever she was going next, to help her fight it.

Her room was neat enough to feel almost unoccupied, but there, on a stand beneath the window, was her suitcase. He went to it, unbuckled the latch, and began to feel around in the pockets, searching—he was not sure for what. A bottle of pills, maybe, or a jar of ointment that he could hold in his hands, the discovery like sliding clothes off her body.

He heard feet on the stairs and knew that Anne-Marie had managed to return without the warning noise he had counted on. He rushed for the door. Towels, he would say. He had been checking to see whether she needed clean towels. He opened the door, and there was Mr. Holbrook's son, Thomas, leaning against the wall and breathing hard from his climb.

Rob recovered himself. "Hello," he said. Thomas was a sad specimen, barely level with Rob's own elbows. Up close his face was pinched and dry looking, his nostrils straining in rapid flexes.

"What're you doing in there?" Thomas said. Rob had thought before that Thomas was six or so, but his voice was unsettling; he was probably closer to ten, just small.

"Mrs. Duncan asked for more towels."

"Mrs. Duncan went into town with my father and that old lady." Thomas wiped his nose with his sleeve. "My father said they'd be gone all morning, and I'm to do my exercises."

"I know. She wanted the towels for when she gets back. You should do them, then, like your father said."

"I won't. It hurts me," Thomas said. He could have been any pouting child except for his face's thinness and his eyes' fevered flash, which somehow raised the stakes on his expression and turned his resentment into real hatred. "Nobody sees how it hurts me."

Rob thought of Thomas's flailing at calisthenics. "They must see."

"Why doesn't somebody *do* something, then?"

Rob's mother was always doing things—running Pilgrim's Inn, and before that the clothes store, and before that the maid service, and before that something else, he was sure, even if he couldn't remember. Yet when he met Thomas's eyes, he understood that none of this was the answer to his question.

BY AFTERNOON IT WAS RAINING, but not hard, just spitting. Rob felt sure that Anne-Marie would still swim. He sat at the front desk for check-in duty and waited. Finally, Anne-Marie walked by in her red suit, her mouth lifting just a little as she passed. He made himself sit for another five minutes, flipping through receipts he'd already sorted, and then sprinted up to his room, stripped, yanked on his swimming trunks, and fled the inn as if it were burning.

Outside, the sky was gray and full of dying light, though it wasn't yet dusk and wouldn't be for hours. The great tide of fog drifting in smelled of the ocean, and it put Rob in a reckless seafaring mood, the kind that gripped the men in his explorer stories and made them stop checking for land behind them. He ran fast enough that there was sweat on his skin by the time he reached the water. She was swimming slowly, straight away from him. No bathing cap today: her wet hair was a dark indiscriminate color, like the head of a seal. Rob blundered into the marsh as fast as he could; he hoped to be covered before she noticed the skinniness of his arms and legs, but the water sucked at his limbs as he lurched around, and when he was at last deep enough for diving, she was facing him.

"Thought it was a nice afternoon for a swim?" Anne-Marie said.

Though the water felt almost the same temperature as the air, it exhaled steam. Rob swam through it with the clumsy back-and-forth of his head that helped propel him forward, out to her. There he could just touch the bottom, and so could she. Her hair clung close to her head and neck, but at the place where it hit the water, it turned liquid, swirling and floating. She was a single arm's length away from him. He could feel his pulse in every part of his body. He knew if he didn't ask now he never would.

"What's actually wrong with you?"

Anne-Marie sighed, and for a moment he expected her to lie again. Instead, she held her arms out in front of her as if asking for an embrace, except her elbows were tucked too close to her body. "My hands," she said.

The pale fingers dripped water while they both looked.

"I can't feel them. I haven't been able to feel them for close to a year. They still mostly move how I want them to, but all the feeling just stops at the wrists. It's not as if I really thought it would do any good, coming here, but..." She shrugged.

That this was all there was to know was incredible to him. He almost grinned. Here he'd been readying himself for battle with something massive and terrifying, and his real opponent was only a pair of numb hands. It was the most genteel problem he had ever heard of. "Really?"

Her face puckered, and she ducked under. He waited for

a long held breath. When she came back up, her face was smoother again, her hair plastered to its sides. "I'm sure it doesn't sound so big," she said. "If you haven't felt it, I guess. But I've been to five doctors. Nobody knows how to stop it." Her voice held the same fury Thomas Holbrook's had.

"Surely someone will figure it out," Rob said, but he no longer felt like grinning. His foot slipped on the muddy bottom, then re-anchored itself.

She blew out with her mouth just above the waterline, showering the space between them with droplets. "You know, Rob, what my husband said when he asked me to marry him? He said I was the only girl in the world who wouldn't slow him down. We'd been children together. Until we were ten, I could run faster than he could. I knew the things he wanted, the places he wanted to see. I only wanted to go with him."

"You did. You went to South America."

She gave a quick shake of her head. "We were in Austria when it started. Charlie'd just finished an assignment, and we'd rented a cabin by some lake. I was getting our supper ready, opening a can of soup. I kept dropping it. I'd pick it up and try to open it and drop it again. I couldn't figure out what was happening. You can't imagine the feeling—it's like trying to do everything through wool mittens. After a while I was crying, but still I worked and worked to get the thing open. And then I looked up, and there was Charlie, watching. The look on his face."

"He should have helped," Rob said. "He should have found help, whatever you needed."

"You're sweet. But Charlie—he's not a bedside sort of person." Anne-Marie pushed the hair off her face with her palms. "The worst part is that some days I'm sure it's moving up. *Advancing*. It will take my wrists and my elbows and my shoulders. Like being frozen to death."

"Let me help," Rob said. Who was more a bedside person than he was? He felt sure that he could help her, that if he could really touch her, all of her, it could change things for both of them. Her problem was only not feeling enough—he knew if he could just show her all he felt, she couldn't help but feel some small portion of it too, even if only as a kind of reflection. He moved closer. "Please," he said.

She looked at him, seeming to consider. He wondered what she was seeing. Then she said, so fast and soft he only barely heard, "Well, you know where my room is. Tonight." And she swam away from him.

ROB WENT BACK TO SIT at the front desk after he'd changed out of his swimming trunks. He told himself that to Anne-Marie he must seem only a boy, that she must be driven by nothing more than the urge to hurt the husband who was off on some mountaintop while she fumbled at the world with her numb hands. She could not want Rob, not in any lasting way. Remembering this, he thought, might help him to keep some hold on himself through the waves of eagerness tumbling him, which he suspected were like those brilliant blue South American waves he'd pictured—not for him.

He glanced up at the framed article. He wondered where the real Betsy was now; the Fosters had moved out of state not long after her recovery, and he'd never seen her in person. He wondered if the cure had lasted. He lifted the frame off its hook. There was the marveling caption, and her face—hard to see clearly in the small photo, but you could tell she was smiling big, as if she'd won something. She still wasn't standing quite straight, but that smile said that it was enough for her, whatever had happened.

At dinner Rob took only a small portion of chicken, and his mother asked him what was wrong.

"Nothing." His insides felt so unsettled that he thought disaster might follow if he put food into them. He'd sat with his back to Anne-Marie, because he knew that otherwise he wouldn't be able to stop looking at her, though by now she had finished eating and gone.

His mother put her hand to his forehead. "You aren't warm."

"I'm fine."

"All right, well, hurry up and eat, please." His mother put a bite of her own chicken into her mouth and talked while she chewed. "I want to let Louise go early tonight, so you're clearing."

"Fine."

"And say a little something to Mrs. Carlson when you take her plate, would you?" He followed her eyes to the old woman he'd checked in just before Anne-Marie. She was staring down at her food as if she didn't quite understand what she was supposed to do with it. "It doesn't have to be much, but it would help. Just say her color's looking better this evening."

"She looks the same to me."

His mother put her fork down and leaned in. "Listen," she whispered, "no one *ever* looks the same. You understand? Pick some little thing you can say is better. Anything you want—it doesn't matter, they'll believe you. They *want* to believe you. You never ever tell them they look the same."

"All *right*," he said.

"We have to work at this, do you understand?" There was something desperate in his mother's face, suddenly, so close to his—and in her voice, though it stayed soft. "Do you know what will happen to us otherwise?"

Rob shook his head. He didn't.

His mother seemed satisfied with this response. She sat back and lifted her fork. "I shouldn't have to tell you these things anymore, Rob. You're not a boy. You'll need to begin pulling some more weight."

In his mind he saw his mother dragging Mrs. Carlson across the dining room floor, lifting one of the old woman's arms, extending it toward him. He stood quickly, feeling sick. "I'm not hungry. I'll start clearing."

"Give that chicken to Louise for her supper, then. That's good chicken."

After, he went to his room and lay on the bed to wait, for how long he wasn't sure. What time had Anne-Marie meant for him to come? It had been maybe an hour since she'd left the dining room; did she need more time than that, to get herself ready somehow? He had no idea how any of this worked. Before him loomed countless undetectable thickets of humiliation into which he might stumble. And yet on a summer afternoon almost three years earlier Betsy Foster had limped into water and walked out again. In spite of Mrs. Carlson and all the others, in spite of everything his mother had used Betsy for since, that one thing had been true. If that could happen, surely he could go into Anne-Marie's room and do what he had promised. There were realms within that room that he had never glimpsed, but surely he could visit them. Before he left his bedroom, he pressed his ears flat against his head, though of course they wouldn't stay.

Outside Anne-Marie's room he stopped, for Thomas sat opposite, cross-legged on the carpet, watching the door.

"Did you get locked out?"

Thomas shook his head. "My father took Mrs. Duncan some dessert. He said I should wait for him in our room. He's been in there a long time." Anne-Marie's laugh floated through the door.

Rob's stomach constricted, as if this revelation were something bitter he had fed to it. He sat on the floor beside Thomas.

"I came back out, though," Thomas said. "I'm going to wait here instead. I want to be here when they come out. I want them to see how they made me wait."

Anticipation of that moment shone on his face. Thomas, Rob realized, would remember this night for years as the time when his father had dessert without him.

How would Anne-Marie remember it? As the time, perhaps, when she had been so full of need that she stepped close to one edge, then turned at the last moment to a different one, with a slightly shorter fall. Mr. Holbrook, he would remember vivid pieces of what was happening behind that door, Anne-Marie's eyes and her mouth, her hands on his skin. He might never know that those hands felt nothing.

And Rob? Rob would remember knowing, as he listened to Thomas wheeze, that Anne-Marie would never open her door for him. He understood that he would watch her leave in a few days, and that he would stay. But he knew, too, that he would still walk past her room every night until she was gone, in case. Just as Anne-Marie herself would go back to the salt marsh in the morning and hold her hands very still below its surface. For a moment, her shoulders would tense, as if she were listening for a sound within herself, a sound she still might hear. Now it could come, now, or now, or now.

AILMENTS

ALL MY LIFE Frances had been hard to bear, but marriage had turned her intolerable. Our mother had taught us about love, speaking the word as if it named an illness and tipping her faded aristocrat's face toward our father as he chewed or scratched his chin—our jowly, thick-fingered father, dust from the road to London worn deep into his knuckle-creases. Understanding as I did the roots of my sister's affliction, though, made me no more inclined to forgive her for it.

I should have been glad that we had gotten Frances married; it had been no sure thing. The match made our father hearty and exultant. I could tell that our mother, who knew more, felt not joy so much as the floating-up relief that comes when a burden is removed from one's arms, an urge to reach toward the sky from which had come this great reprieve. Robert Cresswell was not a man well known to any of us. He had been a physician in London before arriving in our village and had accounted for himself only by saying that he wanted a change of pace, and then that he wanted Frances. I had thought they would set out for somewhere after the marriage—it was evident from the first that he was a man in need of a stage—but they seemed instead to be rooting themselves in place, just a few houses down from our own.

This left Frances free to come and sit and sew with me daily in the same room where we had sewed together for years and interminable years.

"Robert *reads*, you know," Frances told me, one afternoon a few months after the marriage. "He reads all the time. He reads aloud better than anyone I have ever heard."

I could have struck her with the book on the table beside me for all the hours I had read aloud to her in that room. Though our mother had taught us both to read when we were small, somehow Frances, elder of the two of us, had taken to it more slowly, and never fully. When she wanted reading, the duty of providing it had thus fallen, over and over again, to me. The book, a volume of Petrarch, had a good heft; it would have thumped a nice red knot onto that doughy forehead.

"Robert knows so many *people*," Frances said. "They send him letters, from all over. In all sorts of languages. People he knows from his travels. They want his advice about medicine. They want his *ideas*." She raised her eyes from her sewing and widened them at me, muddy ponds reflecting nothing. She looked like a startled cow.

"Impressive," I told her. "Watch your work, though. That dress will thank you for it, and so will your fingers."

"Always the wit," she said, with maternal indulgence, as if she had not lived in mortal fear of that wit for most of her life. Then she seemed to forget me again and sighed the sigh of a woman with a mouthful of her favorite pudding. "He's just so *brilliant*, Cassie."

I listened, as I had to. For the rest of my life I would be listening to Frances. I would like to speak to the soul who could have blamed me for what I felt.

And were there certain features of Dr. Cresswell himself that contributed to my unrest? Would I have preferred that his hat sweep a bit less boldly across his forehead, that his eyes tend more toward dimness? That he sit his horse just slightly less well? That the lines of his legs cut into me not quite so sharply, that they not rise like welts on the surface of my mind as I readied myself for sleep? Yes, yes. Oh yes, that was a part of it, too.

THERE WAS PLAGUE THAT YEAR. In the end its scale would earn it a title: the Great Plague. We could not know that then, but we knew enough to be cautious. Our father hurried home from his law offices in London as fast as he could. He bought pomanders to guard us, and we took care with drafts. Mostly, though, I thought of more immediate miseries. Dr. Cresswell came to collect Frances each afternoon, always well ahead of the summer evening chill. I tried to be elsewhere at these times—upstairs, or in the garden, so that I would not have to watch her redden at the sight of him, an excess of joy that looked like shame.

Sometimes, though, I got the timing wrong. One afternoon in June, he arrived before three o'clock. "You're *early!*" Frances said, voice fraying, when he darkened our doorway.

"It's going to storm." Dr. Cresswell strode into the room with a nod to me. He bowed neatly to kiss her forehead. Then he straightened and surveyed her fondly—it looked like fondly. She dropped her gaze and fussed with the handkerchief she had been stitching, stretching each of the four corners in turn and flattening it on her lap as if to guard her dress from some impending spill. "I wanted to fetch you home before the downpour," he told her. "It seems unlikely you would melt, but I see no need to test the theory. What would become of me if you did?"

I searched for some sign of irony. But the cast of his eyebrows was level and neutral; if his gray eyes screened some joke of his own at Frances's expense, they screened it well.

My sister rose and Dr. Cresswell stood back, well clear of her bustling: the fetching of her hat, the gathering-up of her sewing basket, foldings of cloth and pinnings of pins and a minutes-long hunt for a pattern she had put down *somewhere*, she remembered, she just couldn't remember *where*. Finally it was time for her to fasten her cloak, and she managed to yank one of the buttons right off in her too-eager fingers.

"Cassie!" she cried, holding it up in the air.

I sighed. "Pass it here. I'll tack it back on."

Frances looked out the window at the amassing clouds. "Should I just see if Mother has a pin long enough to fasten it, for now? Why don't I." She rustled out of the room, upsetting her sewing basket in her wake without noticing.

Dr. Cresswell and I eyed the upended basket and then each other. I had never been left alone with him before. He moved first, smoothly. "Allow me," he said as he knelt to the task. He began to sweep things from the floor into the basket. Frances would never be able to find anything in there.

"Many thanks." I cleared my throat, then regretted having done so, since it had the sound of a preamble. I sought refuge in sewing and watched my own fingers fumble on the cloth.

"You're welcome, sister. Cassandra." He looked up at me. "A fanciful sort of name, Cassandra, is it not? An unusual choice, given the unhappy fate of the namesake. You know, of course...?"

I could feel the flush of my cheeks, and filled with a violent disdain for the quivery self he was turning me into. I wondered when exactly I had fallen victim to this affliction, what weakness of mine had allowed it entrance. "Of course," I said shortly.

My reply did nothing to quell Dr. Cresswell's enthusiasm. Finished by now with the sewing basket, he stood upright, one hand tented on his chest, a rhetorical pose. "I always have thought we ought to attend more closely to those old stories. All of life is in them. The Fall of Troy, the fate of Priam. The hurling of children from the battlements. So will great civilizations always end." He began to pace across our small flowered carpet. His free hand swung a little. "We live our lives with a foolish illusion of permanence. We prefer to remain ignorant, even when such ignorance requires the deliberate aversion of our gaze. There are many kinds of fire, but always fire, in the end."

I thought of several possible retorts, each of which would have been satisfying. I might have told him that my education lay outside the province of his responsibilities. Or observed that this was hardly a new idea he was voicing so proudly, as if he had just now birthed it glimmering from his brain. Any of these might have made him see that he was not so impressive to me as he appeared to be to himself. But there were too many possibilities, and they tangled before I could choose among them.

There was also the physical fact of him there across the narrow room, stepping, it seemed to me, a bit higher than needed, taking visible delight in the spring and catch of muscle and tendon, mouth flexing. How was I to bear his closeness? The room's humid air felt thick against my face. We both turned to the window as the first fat drops of rain hit the glass. His fingertips still pressed to his chest the way a man touches a treasure.

That touch made me want, above all things, to touch him too.

With a fast and heavy tread, Frances was back in the room.

"All pinned!" she said breathlessly. "Let's go before the rain gets any worse, shall we, love?"

Love, they often called each other, naming the force and not the person in question, as if it had become the only important thing about either of them.

There was some relief in their departure, some cooling of my cheeks, but it did not last. I wished he would not try to talk to me. It made me think of his talking to my sister, his talking to her while lying in their bed. That mouth of his would be drawn up in its teaching posture, relishing the shape of each word. Frances would relish, too; Frances would run her fingertips over those shapes, which would seem to her extraordinary. Only I could not for the life of me see how this could be enough for him. She would have nothing to say in response. There would be nothing she could offer but to press her own thin lips—no lips at all, almost—to his.

WHEN WE WERE CHILDREN, Frances and I, our mother had a custom of reading aloud to us from Scripture in the afternoons. At the reading's end she would elucidate what we had heard, fashioning small, direct lessons for use in our own lives. The lessons were what one might expect: the rewards of kindness, the dangers of pride. I took them to heart, or tried to. In those days there was a part of me that wanted very much to be kind to Frances, especially kind, and smooth away the world's roughness for her—though always there was another part that held her in scorn, and myself for doing so.

On a morning when I was perhaps twelve, Frances fourteen, our reading brought us to the story of Jacob and Rachel, at the well and after. His working for her all that time, only to earn the unwanted Leah; his continued working for, at last, the desired sister. Our mother read the story more quickly than usual, then set the book aside.

"Well?" I said. "The moral, mother?" I felt both excited

and afraid. I suspected that some cloudy thing I had long sensed, without being able to name it, would now be forced into the light. Now our mother would have to give it words.

Frances turned her eyes to the floor.

Our mother fixed me with a level gaze. "Sometimes," she said, "a story is only a story."

I have often thought that the story of our whole lives, Frances's and mine, is somewhere in that line.

THE SUMMER GREW HOTTER; the air stilled. One morning as we sewed, Frances pulled a long, black, waxy garment out of her basket and spread it across her knees. She found its tear, all down one of its seams, in an unhurried way—careful, I thought, not to look at me.

"What is that, Frances?"

"An old overcoat of Robert's. Needs mending."

But I knew what it was, that thing with its oily fish-skin gleam. I had seen drawings of the black-garbed men with the heads of birds in the pamphlets our father sometimes brought home with him. It was a plague doctor's coat. Dr. Cresswell must still be riding into London to attend the sick, then. He would have the bird-mask too, somewhere, that talisman against the bad air.

Frances must have wanted me to see, to know. She was peddling one more of her husband's impressive features. I would not buy, I determined; I would not ask her a thing.

I picked up my stitch just where I had left it, and my needle was even as it bit-slid, bit-slid; but all the while I was picturing Dr. Cresswell's eyes, fierce, clear, and diagnostic, above the mask's beak. When Frances left the room I reached out to touch the coat's gummed surface, to which the flesh of my fingers stuck.

Reports of the plague's spread came daily. By midsummer our father was putting off all the clients he could, limiting his trips to London; when he returned from meeting those who'd insisted, his face had an inward cast, and we knew better than to ask what he had seen. We were thankful to be out in the country, but there was fear in the gratitude, a feeling that our safety could not last. Fear in everyone—all but Frances, who still hummed tuneless little songs, whose skin still seemed moist with joy.

In the homes of the sick—who were also, almost always, the dying—Dr. Cresswell would be witnessing horrors. Of these I had only the vaguest of ideas, but I could envision clearly the way he would seem to his patients: a looming dark bird-shape made mythic by fever. I looked out the window at night and imagined I could see his black-clothed figure hovering there, watching me, the coat clinging to all the lean lines of him. I imagined what would happen if I were to go to the window and let that figure in. Perhaps the beak was not a mask at all but real, real sharpness, with the capacity to hurt if I forgot myself for even a moment.

But the bird had flown to Frances and not to me. She had become the proprietor of that visitation, a thing that seemed to me as improbable as flight itself.

AT CHURCH ON A SUNDAY IN JULY, the hottest day yet, we were offered Holy Communion. The vicar held the cup out to Dr. Cresswell, who told him, "No, thank you."

He had brushed against me inadvertently as we'd entered the church, and I was still so full of the inflaming thrill of that whisper, cloth on cloth, that it took me a moment to hear his words. Frances, beside me in the women's section, sucked in a wet breath. Dr. Cresswell had accepted the bread readily enough, and the vicar continued to thrust the cup toward his lips, brow slightly furrowed. Our vicar had been an old man for as long as I could remember. His hands, and the cup in them, trembled.

"No, thank you," Dr. Cresswell repeated. Not loud, but loud enough to be heard in the silence of the sanctuary. If all he had wanted was not to taste, he might have simply crossed his arms and bowed his head, as the others who'd refused communion for private matters of conscience had done. But this was aimed at all of us.

Our mother's lips tightened. "What is he doing?" she asked Frances, and me, too, as if the two of us were equally responsible. Beside Dr. Cresswell in the pew, our father stifled the laughter that always claimed him when he was at a loss.

"Lowering the risk of contagion," Dr. Cresswell said. The men's and women's sections were divided only by a narrow aisle—ours was a small church—but still, to have heard my mother, he must have been watching for our reaction. "There is fresh thinking on this matter, a reinspection of the old," he continued. "Understand, I would never do this lightly. The newest theory is that to put one's mouth where the mouths of others have been in a time of plague is a foolish danger."

"The *Holy Communion*, Robert," Frances said, barely above a whisper—so strange it must have felt to her to be talking in church. She looked like a woman whose beautiful new dress, in which she had delighted, had ripped unexpectedly.

"I explained this to you, Frances," Dr. Cresswell told her.

"But," Frances said, then stopped. I knew what she was thinking. She hadn't expected that when the moment came, he would really make such a scene.

"You may choose for yourself, my love," Dr. Cresswell told her. "But I must urge you to consider, to fully consider. Would God want you to risk yourself in this way?"

Frances looked at the cloth with which the vicar had wiped the rim of the cup between the sips of the faithful. My eyes went with hers, to those pink stains, then back to Dr. Cresswell.

"All right," Frances said. She crossed her arms and bowed her head.

Dr. Cresswell watched the watching people. Each of them would be starting to wonder about the risk. I could see already the shape this moment would assume in Frances's sewing-room retellings, which would be endless: *You remember, Cassie, his bravery, his wisdom.* Dr. Cresswell's lips seemed on the very verge of opening again to deliver more words and tip what hung in the balance here in his favor. Of course Dr. Cresswell preferred not to press his mouth to the cup's edge, as if his were anyone else's. My face burned.

"I know what I will choose," I said loudly, for I could talk to the listening people too. "I will observe the sacrament."

My words set the vicar back in motion. He moved down the line to my father, and his hands settled into the easy ruts of his routine: raise the cup, touch it to the waiting lips, tip the liquid down the throat. When he came to me, the wine bloomed in my mouth and then in my stomach.

THE SCENE REPEATED ITSELF. Each time my parents and I took the sacrament, along with the rest of the village; each time Dr. Cresswell and my sister did not, and our neighbors stared. I felt sure that I had put some of the judgment into those stares.

Frances was not cut from sturdy enough cloth to make a good religious rebel. Other people's anger had always withered her. When she was ten and I was eight and she accidentally left my favorite poppet out in the rain—my life is strewn with the wreckage of Frances's accidents—she cried for twice as long as I did, then gave me her own favorite in recompense.

No real recompense was possible now. The one act that would have pleased those she had offended would have betrayed her husband. Her flesh seemed to droop as the days passed; her eyes became rheumy. She began to avoid our sewing times, coming only every third day or so, which suited me. When she did come, she brought word of letters upon letters from people of Dr. Cresswell's acquaintance who approved of his course. She recited the names with desperation. "Another letter from Dr. Littleham, just yesterday," she told me. "Saying again that Robert is right."

"How pleasing for the both of them," I said. I thought she might cry.

Meanwhile, Dr. Cresswell himself seemed to have taken me on as a personal mission. He did not bother much with my parents; perhaps he sensed the futility of that pursuit, or perhaps he thought that if he won me, I might deliver them as well, and any number of others. In any case he seemed to need to explain himself again and again, to someone. He often came to see me on the days when Frances did not. He always began by making apologies for my sister's absence.

"No need," I told him.

"Frances is unwell."

"Isn't that odd?"

He exhaled, plainly furious. I gave him a pleasant smile. The project of defying him had contented me beyond what I had foreseen; I felt more composed than ever before, and hard—a beatific, rounded marble statue.

He rearranged his face and spread his hands. "I have nothing but respect for your faith, Cassandra."

"Thank you," I said.

"But let me say it once more. This is the very latest thinking."

"Certainly we must be current."

"You accept, I trust, that if you were to touch with your tongue a thing that had been covered in paint, the paint would be transferred to your mouth? Why should disease not work in the same way? It is surely caused by physical agents. Contact with the ill, or contact with sites with which they have been in contact, is a means of opening oneself to their disease."

The wave of plague had come to feel as large and abstract, as unlikely to touch my life, as the faith Dr. Cresswell had mistakenly attributed to me—whereas I knew my other sickness could reclaim me in an instant, though my refusal to heed him had armed me, for now, against it. I raised my eyebrows. "I see."

"You do *not* see. It is not possible that you see." His hand clenched now in the air between us. "How close have you been to a person dying of the plague?"

He had been as close as it was possible to be, of course. This thought raised the great black bird in my mind to flight again and took away my lovely marbly feeling.

Dr. Cresswell did not seem to have noticed my change. "It is a thing," he said, "too terrible to describe to a person as young as you are."

I looked at him curiously. I did not feel young.

My mother entered the room then. She stopped short when she saw Dr. Cresswell. "Oh," she said, "I hadn't realized you'd come."

He inclined his head. "I hope you're enjoying the morning."

"We're working through the ledger books." She and my father did this at the close of every week. She would have left my father red-faced, peering down at the small black markings that noted the particulars of suits and fees, and that so often seemed to turn on him. She would have fled that room, telling him that she needed something—an old record book, a shawl—when what she really needed, I knew, was air.

I saw a sketch, once, that my mother drew of my father when she first knew him. He strides through a field with his dog at his heels. He looks like a young king gone hunting.

"The work goes smoothly, I hope?" Dr. Cresswell said.

"It goes much as it always goes." She adjusted her sleeve at the wrist. "Do tell Frances we'd love to see her later on. She comes less often than we would like nowadays."

I almost laughed; I only just stopped myself.

"She's had much to occupy her," Dr. Cresswell told us.

"I thought you said she was unwell?" I said.

"In any case," said my mother quickly. "Please just tell her that we miss her."

Dr. Cresswell nodded. "Well, I won't keep you," he said.

I cast my gaze out the window, as he left, so that my mother would not see me looking after him. "I wonder," I remarked, "if it may soon rain."

"NO FRANCES AGAIN?" my mother said, wiping fine beads of sweat from her upper lip on a Thursday morning in August.

"It seems not."

"We haven't seen her all week."

"Are you complaining?"

"Cassandra," she said, reprovingly.

"Yes?" It had been an honest question. I couldn't understand why she wouldn't take the tapering of my sister's visits as the great sparing it was to me.

"You ought to be kinder," she told me. "Your gifts and Frances's are different. You ought to appreciate hers as she does yours."

As if I needed to be told we were different. I could see the mark of this difference in almost every memory I had. It was there in all her blunders; in all the times the girls in our village left me alone, because to include me would have been to include her too; in all the subtle curbing of our learning at our mother's hands, so that Frances should not feel the pangs of being left behind; in the thousand small conversations at our table that stopped short at the point past which she would have been unable to trace them. Frances's limitations had always been mine as well. The rage in me stirred.

"*Gifts?*" I said.

"Yes, gifts. And Frances needs our appreciation and our caring just now, more than ever. Her position is—not easy." My mother's lips parted and she dabbed them again with her handkerchief. "Marriage isn't simple, Cassandra. Someday you will understand." She sighed, shifting in her chair. "Walk over and see how your sister is, won't you?" she asked.

IN THE LANE BETWEEN OUR HOUSES, dust clung to the hem of my skirt. The day's heat was a kind of stupor. Even the leaves of the trees were limp; they looked as fat and wet as eating-greens. I kicked a stone and watched it tumble away from me. I wished I had told my mother she need not speak to me about the complexity of a thing Frances had grasped, but the fact remained, indisputable, that Frances and not I had grasped it.

The cottage where my sister and her husband lived had the blank-eyed look of a slow child. I knocked, hard. "Frances," I said. "Frances, Mother's worried." I knocked again, then turned the knob.

Inside, it was darker but not much cooler, the air just as thick as without. "Frances," I called, "Frances?" I moved slowly across the floor, feeling the boards' slight shift beneath my feet. If this were my house, I thought, if this were the house of my marriage, I would know the give of each of these boards by heart.

These would be my stairs that I was climbing now, my footsteps soft and easy. This would be my bedroom door, half ajar, that I was pushing open. My room whose center I stood in. Mine and my husband's together.

I had entered this room before when visiting Frances—though I did not visit often—but it was something different to be in it without her. It was close and hot and smelled of sleep. The bed was neatly made, with the same tuck at the corners that Frances had given her bed linens as a girl. I seated myself on it. My new angle brought my gaze to the long black coat Frances had mended, hanging over a chair.

On the floor, protruding from between the folds, was the beak of the mask.

I stilled. Then I stood and approached. I touched the coat, which seemed in its sloppy drape to preserve the haste of the arm that had thrown it, and was as warm as sleeping skin. I lifted the mask toward me, lighter than I had imagined, a clumsy homemade thing of stained and stiff brown leather. Its eyes were dull red glass, one webbed in small cracks. Down the beak ran a line of stitches. A mouth sewn closed but smiling slyly. I was touching it, holding it, but I wanted to be closer still.

I put on the coat first, heavy and so long it fell almost to the floor. The weight of it dragged on my shoulders. I reached again for the mask and settled it over my head. A soft red hazed the room. Because the mask did not fit close against my skin I had light enough to see that there were herbs inside the beak, shriveled as an old woman's dried bridal flowers. They had a salty, tangy smell. My shoulders, my chest, my mouth were all where Dr. Cresswell's had been. My sister, wife or no, had never stood inside him, in the very heart of him. I put out my tongue to taste the papery leaves.

Frances's voice came from behind me.

"Oh, Robert," Frances said.

Then, "Oh, love."

"I had thought you were feeling better," she said.

She ought to have seen that I was too slight to be her husband, beneath that coat, under that mask. I have never been able to understand why she did not see this.

Frances came closer. Her eyes were sad and wary. She reached one hand toward me, very slowly, as if she feared I might bolt. "I was out back in the garden. I thought you had gone to Essex. Robert, Mr. Allen's expecting you."

What could I say? I said nothing.

"What was it, love?" Frances said, after enough time had

passed to show that I would not answer. "What was it this time?" Her voice held a vast, weary patience. "Did someone cough in the street on the way?"

What could I do? I could not speak. I inclined my long beak toward her.

Frances seemed to take my silence for assent. "But I have told you. There's no plague, not here, so you're safe. You don't need that thing anymore. You know you don't. We aren't in London. You need never go back there."

Her hand was on my shoulder now. She stroked it down my arm. "You need to put it away. Haven't you told me so yourself? You've been doing so well."

Frances waited. She was a woman I did not know, who had delivered these lines many times before and who expected to be obeyed. I had to stop my hands from reaching up to remove the mask as she had instructed.

Frances closed her eyes and opened them again. "Well," she said. "Give yourself some time, then, love. When you feel better again, calmer, take it off and come out to the garden. We'll talk then. All right?"

And what if I never feel better? I wanted to ask her. Frances, what if I never do?

Before she turned to go, she rested her hand for a moment on my elbow and smiled. I had never before seen a smile like that. I would not have believed that my sister's lips could carry so much. It was a smile to be used at a sickbed, and in it was a life of ardent, hopeless tending, her embrace of Dr. Cresswell's sickbed as her own.

What had I known about the heart of anything?

It would transpire that these were the same moments in which Anna Peterson, down the street, was seized by a chill. "There's a draft," she said to her husband, but in truth it did not feel quite like a draft; it felt less transient, more intentional, as if a tight pocket of winter had enveloped her there in her over-warm sitting room and would stay for some time.

She shuddered, rose, and went to her bedroom, thinking to lie down. Her maid, helping her to undress, was the first to see the hot red lump at the side of Anna's neck. Anna fingered the swelling and screamed.

The maid would tell us that it looked as if Anna's heart were trying to crawl out her throat.

I was silent, in the Cresswells' marriage bedroom, silent but quick as I took off the coat and mask and put them back where I had found them. I could be done with this, I told myself—done as Frances never could be. The unhealthy heart that beat in this room, I could leave it behind. It was not mine.

But as I stole down the stairs and out the door, I thought of the way the mask had tangled in my hair when I lifted it over my head, and my own heart thudded. I wondered if a strand might have caught and remained. When next he put on the mask, I wondered if it might brush against his skin, against his mouth, if, for just a moment, he might taste me there.

WE SHOW WHAT WE HAVE LEARNED

Before her disintegration, we had long held an absolute and unwavering contempt for Ms. Swenson. She had won that with her uncertainty, which we had sensed in the very first moments of our very first day of fifth grade, the way dogs can smell fear. Waves of it rolled off her, along with the odor of cats and Kleenex and chalk that hung, unsurprisingly, in her sad, pilly sweaters. Ms. Swenson was pitiful, but this did not mean we pitied her. We felt nothing for the faded blue of her eyes, which were like a sea creature's soft underbelly, or for the way she kept them open so wide and blinked so rapidly that she seemed to be seeing us through a mist. Her movements, too, were misty, whereas we were sharp and quick and feral. We did not wonder much about her life. She seemed ageless to us in the way that most adults seemed ageless—we could not have said whether she was twenty-five or forty—but we did know that she was younger than most of the other teachers. This was less because her face was unlined than because she seemed so much more un-finished. Everything Ms. Swenson ever said to us had a ques-tion in it, even when she explained long division or poetry, things it was clear she understood and loved, and even when she told Mark Peters to stop it when he pulled down Sally Winters's pants and underpants to show us the hair-flecked space between her legs. The question in her voice then was simply more panicked than usual.

The day the disintegration began, we were learning about Native American civilization. We were always learning about Native American civilization—we began each year with it, and then we might, as on that day, when we were supposed to be talking about the Civil War, make several unexpected detours back to revel in the quietude of that life so close to nature. The teachers all loved these lost things—vanished ways of life, great men who died early, extinct animals—and Ms. Swenson loved them even more than most. We watched while she drew a wigwam on the board. Ms. Swenson was very bad at drawing, worse even than the worst of us, because she was crippled by second guessing. She darted in to draw a line, darted back to look at it, darted back in to erase it and start over. "Is that straight?" she asked us, but wasn't it supposed to be rounded, wasn't that the whole point? Finally she sighed in a way that meant she was giving up and settling for the misshapen thing she had produced. "You see, children, the *hole* was put there," she said, pointing, "so that the cooking smells could escape. It's *ingenious.*" Her hands began to wave desperately and hopelessly, as if she were trying to breathe with them, like vestigial gills. There was something beautiful about her excitement in these moments, irresistible target though it was. "The early colonists were *never* so ingenious.

In many ways, the civilization they would *brutally* overpower was *vastly* superior to their own."

Abner Harris raised his hand. Ms. Swenson never did learn not to call on him. Perhaps she was distracted by the glimmering vision of wigwams in her mind, a whole village of them where she might have lived gently and happily in our absence. Tending plants, fetching water from the stream, watching smoke rise toward bright stars. "Yes, Abner?" Ms. Swenson said.

"Is that what holes are always there for?"

"Is *what* what they're always there for, Abner?"

"So smells can escape? Is that what, like, Rachel's hole is there for?"

"Rachel's hole?" Ms. Swenson said, musingly, still failing to understand, though Rachel was already blushing. When Ms. Swenson got there, two red spots appeared high on her cheeks. "Abner, that is inappropriate," she said and yet managed to sound as if she were asking for permission to reprimand him.

"What is?"

Mock innocence was mortally wounding to her; she couldn't help taking it at face value. We waited, snuffling into our hands and tasting the salt of our palms, chewing on the skin around our fingernails with the glee of what was coming.

"To *speak* about the..." she flopped like a speared fish, "private parts of others."

"But Ms. Swenson," said Billy Nichols, drawn to the blood in the water, "which parts *are* private? I forget."

We squeaked our sweaty hands against our desks in joy. Now she would have to *say* them, *say* those words. What could be more wonderful? We would hear them from her lips.

And that was when it happened. We would wonder, ever after, what caused it: the force of the bottled-up, forbidden words we were calling forth or the hammering blows of the humiliation we were delivering. Whether the force came from within or without. Ms. Swenson, in her agitation, flicked her webby hair behind her ear, chalk still in hand, and in the process flicked some object off herself. It flew forth with so much force that the act would have seemed intentional but for the puzzlement on her face. An earring, we assumed, at first. But the earrings Ms. Swenson wore were not as large as this.

Hannah Perkins, in the first row, began to scream. She was peering over the edge of her desk at the thing on the floor, and she curled her feet up under her as if to keep them away from a mouse. We left our seats and clustered around the space in front of Hannah's desk.

The thing on the ground was an earlobe.

Detached, it looked very fleshy, though Ms. Swenson had never before seemed to have especially fleshy ears. It sat on the ground like a fat, self-satisfied grub, one that had perhaps eaten its brethren. Ms. Swenson's small gold hoop earring was still in place, puckering the roundest part of the lobe's belly. There was no blood; there was simply one ragged edge. Naturally, we looked from there to the rest of Ms. Swenson's still-attached ear, the matching puzzle piece, the yin to the lobe's yang. No blood there either—the gap made us queasy, but it seemed more the result of a shedding than of a wound. Then we looked at her face.

"Hmm," Ms. Swenson said. She turned away. We thought she might begin to scream. Instead she went calmly to her desk, swished a tissue from its box, and returned to the lobe on the carpet. She covered it with the tissue, and for a second it seemed she might leave it there, a small sheet over a small corpse. Then, with an expression of distaste, she reached out and lifted it just as she might have lifted a dog turd. She walked back to her desk, opened the drawer, and placed the lobe inside. She shut the drawer softly. Only then did she look at us. She seemed to have just remembered where she was.

"I can trust you, I think," she said, "not to mention this to anyone." We were surprised by the lack of a question in her voice.

Our classroom was quieter than it had ever been. If she planned for this to stay a secret somehow, we would not give her away. We nodded, twenty-six heads in unison, the first grown-up promise we had ever made, one of the few some of us would ever keep.

"Now," said Ms. Swenson, "I believe we were discussing the wigwam."

HERE ARE THE PARTS that Ms. Swenson lost in the days that followed: three molars, the end of her nose, a chunk of one shoulder, which she shook from her sleeve, her lower lip, and assorted fingers and toes, including all of the fingers of her right hand except the thumb. She still managed to hold the chalk by pinning it between thumb and palm. Her penmanship didn't look much different than usual. We applauded this triumph, literally applauded it with our shamelessly whole hands, and she acknowledged the tribute with a nod before continuing with the lesson. There was something different about her lessons now. We were attending to them anew, horrified, rapt. Ms. Swenson was not a dramatically better teacher than she had been before—she still apologized and bobbled, though the missing lower lip gave her an irritated expression—but we were dramatically better students. We wondered which words would move her enough to move a piece off of her, and the wondering made us really listen to those words, which made us learn from them, in most cases for the first time. We learned to multiply and divide large numbers gracefully, to conjugate French verbs, to spell "ambiguity"; we learned the order of Civil War battles and the types of rocks—igneous, metamorphic, sedimentary. This progress was so painless it was scarcely noticeable to us. In becoming a mystery, Ms. Swenson had gained our devotion. Our love and our fear of her grew in direct proportion to the little sheeted mounds in her desk drawers. One day at recess, Tom Milk brought out a tissue bundle he said he had stolen from the desk; he claimed it was the left index finger we had seen her shed two days earlier. His reluctance to let us see it was a tell, though, and when Shawn Greggors seized it from him and shook it out, nothing but more tissues emerged to dance away across the pavement. You could not have paid us, any of us, to touch the genuine relics.

It was a month from the first earlobe to the culmination. We had suspected some end must be nearing—*What can be left?* we'd whispered—but still we were unprepared.

Ms. Swenson was explaining the mating rituals of frogs. "The male gives a little call like this: *whoo whoooo.*" She sounded more like an owl. She crouched down to approximate a frog with her carriage. "He tries to call as loud as he can. The female hears the call and thinks, *Oh my, what's that?* And then she gives a little hop."

This was where Ms. Swenson forgot her limitations and gave a little hop of her own to demonstrate. It was a small hop, but it was enough. In addition to the thump of her weight as her feet hit the ground, there was a sound like wet cloth tearing. Both of her legs detached somewhere near the hips and fell away beneath her skirt. Her torso plummeted. "Oof," she said with the impact. Her shoulders separated from her chest. Her head separated from her neck and landed facedown on the carpet.

There was a silence.

"Okay," Ms. Swenson said. Her voice was carpet muffled, bright with effort. "That wasn't so bad. Not as bad as I thought it would be. Stephanie?" Stephanie was the girl at whose socks Ms. Swenson was now staring. "Stephanie, would you please put me on that chair?"

Stephanie did not want to touch the head, we could all see

this, but how do you refuse a request like that? She picked Ms. Swenson up, holding her far away from her own body, and carried her toward a chair at the front of the room. She had to step over Ms. Swenson's torso to get there, and she looked down, seeming to consider and then dismiss the possibility that she was responsible for it too. "At least that's over," Ms. Swenson said en route.

When Stephanie put her down, though, we could tell it wasn't over yet. A great hunk of Ms. Swenson's hair came away in Stephanie's hand; Stephanie shrieked softly and brushed it off against her pants, where it clung for a moment before falling to the floor. Ms. Swenson didn't seem to notice. As we watched, one of her eyebrows lifted from her face like peeling paint and fell in a curl to the seat of the chair. Her upper lip was starting to look crooked. "Children, we must be quick, now," Ms. Swenson said. "It is time for you to show what you have learned."

We misunderstood her at first. We rummaged frantically for pencils and paper. Some of us set to work multiplying and dividing; others began to spell out previously elusive words. Still others began lists of facts. We could have filled pages and pages with those facts. We could have wallpapered the classroom with them.

"Not *that*!" Ms. Swenson said. We looked up at her. An eyelid slipped its moorings. "Is that all you know? Is that all I have taught you?" Her panic had set the eyeball beneath the crazily hung eyelid rolling; we wondered if she could still see out of it.

We waited for her to regain her composure and tell us again what we were to do. We wanted to please her as much as we had ever wanted anything.

"You must see," she said. "It's your turn, children. You'll have to, you know. And haven't I been demonstrating for weeks now? Haven't you been paying attention? All of you ought to know by now how it is done."

Those of us who had understood were hoping we hadn't. Ms. Swenson's patience had run out. "Show me, children!" she screamed. "Come apart!"

But the force of that *p* was too much; it blew her upper lip clear off. Her gaze followed it as it sailed away from her, hit the edge of Stephanie's desk, and stuck, and she seemed to surrender. We had thought the finale would be spectacular. We had been waiting for days for her eyes to pop cartoonishly, for her to fling a moist slab of tongue toward us. These things did not happen. She just gave a sigh, and her head sank to one side a little, and that was all.

All except for the feelings we felt next.

It began differently for each of us, Ms. Swenson's final lesson. Some of us felt it gathering in the tiny bird-bones of our fingers, some in our hard, pink, healthy gums. For some, it came first to the pristine joints of our vertebrae. For still others, it settled in the unobstructed tunnels, lustrous and smooth, that led into and out of our childish and unscarred hearts. But though it took so many different forms, the beginning was universal. Not even the most whole among us was exempt. You would not have seen a difference to look at us, but we had changed, were changing, as our seams learned how to loosen. We were becoming divisible. We would come to understand that in this way, Ms. Swenson had prepared us.

For the future is gated, and there are tolls to be paid.

THE DROP

THE CHURCH LADIES were having coffee in the living room of the Baker house when Martin Williams delivered his parachute to Lily Baker, his bride. Only some of the church ladies could really have been there, but in retellings they all claimed seats. They allowed one another this. A natural desire, to be part of the story.

At his knock, Lily flitted to the door to show him in, flushed with pleasure. Who could blame her, the way he looked in the uniform he still wore everywhere? Martin was only newly home, and Lily liked new things. But her face fell a little when he set his sack down at his feet and pulled the silk from it in a long, thick rope.

"That's it?" she said.

They'd all known the parachute was coming. Martin had brought it back with him in order to furnish a wedding dress for his bride. This was an uncommon but not unprecedented idea among the men who were returning. To the church ladies it made some sense: bringing one kind of attachment to bear on another.

A strong attachment, in Martin's case. He'd made it clear the dress was as fundamental as the bride herself to the vision he had of his wedding day. This vision seemed to be very clear-etched for that of a man.

Martin snapped the chute in the air, laying it out on Emma Baker's carpet. Pride in his wrists.

Emma grasped her daughter's arm. "Oh, Lily," she breathed, the sort of ineffectual thing Emma was always breathing.

"Saved my life," Martin said. He bent and floated his fingertips along the parachute's stiff skin, the way he might have caressed a lovely woman's cheek. "My wife should be so lucky." He laughed a screaming sort of laugh that was not quite so dashing as the figure he cut in that nice crisp uniform, then said to Lily, "I can't wait to see you both coming toward me down the aisle."

He relayed a question from his mother about the reception hall; Emma told him to ask his mother, in turn, about the side dishes. The church ladies had their own opinions on both matters, which they swallowed, for now.

Martin turned toward the door. In some physical way, he seemed to have trouble leaving the parachute behind.

"Be good to her." He gave a split-wide smile.

"Her?" Lily said, but he was already out the door.

The church ladies closed in on the parachute, reaching to touch it. Going down on their knees on the carpet wasn't easy.

"It's silk at least. Not that nylon some of them are made from," somebody said.

Lily knelt with the others, brushed it with her fingers, then drew her hand back.

"If I have to wear it I will die," she hissed to her mother, loud enough for everyone to hear.

But what did Lily know about dying? They all remembered half a year earlier, when she'd sworn with equal fervor that the cruel lack of a party for her high school graduation—the absence of records and dancing—would kill her. When there'd been no party, some of the ladies had pointed out to her that she seemed to have gone on living, and she'd sulked like the child she was. It was Emma's fault, the ladies thought. She'd always been too soft with Lily, who was in this case likely just reacting to the scrim of the cheap silk, to the way a fingernail whiskered unpleasantly against it.

"At least it feels," one of them told her, "like something *living* made it."

A MONTH LATER Emma and Lily went with Martin's mother, Sarah Williams, to Mrs. Bolland's seamstress shop to see the transformation. Lily couldn't seem to stop talking in the car on the way over. "I bet she will have had to use a lot of new material," she said from the backseat, the words pitched high. "Mostly new material, probably."

Emma wished Lily would be still. Sarah Williams, silent in the passenger seat, had always struck Emma as intimidatingly stoical. Lily's tinny chatter seemed a chink in Emma's own armor.

Lily had quieted down as they parked the car and entered the shop, and by the time Mrs. Bolland bustled forth and ushered them back to the try-on room, Lily would look at nothing but the carpet. This too, though, was humiliating. Emma and Gary had taught Lily manners—Emma could recall many small and skillful moments of such teaching over the years—but you would never have known. "Come with me, honey, and let's get you into it," Mrs. Bolland said. She took Lily's arm in one squared-off workman's hand.

Emma felt embarrassed she'd needed to hire those hands, when Martin had likely been picturing some scene of homey living-room sewing, busy fingers flickering in firelight. For a moment, Emma felt sure that Lily would dig her heels in and refuse to budge. But her daughter's feet tripped after Mrs. Bolland tractably enough.

Mrs. Bolland took Lily behind a screen and there were rustlings of fabric, thuds of shoes striking the floor. "I think you'll be happy with how it turned out," Mrs. Bolland said. "I gathered it all nice." Not a sound from Lily; you would have thought Mrs. Bolland was back there alone. "All right," she said at last, and led Lily out to stand in the center of the room.

The dress wasn't bad-looking, in Emma's opinion. It didn't look much like a parachute unless you had your eyes peeled for the resemblance. The white of it dazzled, as white does. Mrs. Bolland had given it pretty sleeves with points at the wrists, a drop waist that made Lily look streamlined and almost elegant, like something turned on a lathe. Also a fetching neckline, dipping to a V, just low enough, framing the collarbone. What was least pleasing about that silk was its feel, and how many would really be laying hands on it at the wedding? There did seem to be a slightly unusual volumi- nousness to the skirt, especially noticeable in motion, as if the thing could not quite forget how to catch the air—somehow this gave Lily an unsettling appearance of leglessness—but mostly it looked like anyone's wedding dress. The whole effect was just fine.

Do you see? Emma wanted to say to her daughter. Do you see how it's not so bad? He comes back from over there and asks only this of you—what else could you possibly tell him? But she could not seem to catch Lily's eye.

THE DAY OF THE WEDDING ARRIVED, wet and warm for November. The mothers planned to put Lily into the dress in the minister's room off the vestibule of the church. "I think today you need it more than I do," he told them jovially.

Lily Baker, on this, her last day of being Lily Baker, made no effort to smile back at Reverend Barris. She knew it was the mothers he was smiling for anyway, that they were who he had to please, really.

Inside, the door shut, Lily was seized with a need to have the thing over and done with as quickly as possible. She took off her blouse and stepped out of her green woolen skirt before the mothers had put their things down or turned their attention to the dress in its garment bag and waited in her slip, divested of her coverings, for the dress to reach the same naked state.

Mrs. Williams took it from the bag. She draped it across her knees to set to work on the buttons. Lily had thought herself ready, but at the sight of the dress, her panic returned. It was possible, when not in the same room with it, for Lily to convince herself she was exaggerating her own feelings, a tendency not foreign to her. She had been thinking that even this morning when she awoke with dread curling her toes. This is your wedding day, she had told herself sternly (trying to employ her mother's voice for the purpose). It's a pretty enough dress, and it's a dress to be worn once. You're just disappointed it's not how you imagined—a froth of lacy newness for everyone to see you in.

But now there it was, right across from her, and disappointed was not the word for what Lily felt. The dress was every inch as bad as it was possible for a dress to be. It had such a terrible, gleeful gleam, beckoning the touch malevolently, and then how repellent its feel on the fingers. And all this was nothing compared to the smell, which Lily could not smell now, not yet. She had first smelled it on that day months ago when Martin had snapped the parachute in the air and laid it out on the living-room floor, as if introducing Lily to a third party entitled to all wedding considerations.

Her. Only a very slight smell, sour, one Lily couldn't quite place or name, but somehow it had crowded everything else out of her head. She knew now that smell was only waiting.

Her mother eyed Lily critically. "You won't be needing that slip," she said. "The material's thick enough."

"Just to be sure," Lily said. She hoped she sounded reasonable. She would not have the dress right up against her skin. She would not. She hadn't been successful in making anyone understand her feelings and so she would wear this dress, but she would sooner run shrieking from the room than feel its slippery skin against her bare stomach. Let them try her.

"You're going to be so hot," her mother said, but Mrs. Williams looked up from the buttons she was still undoing and said, "Oh, let her wear the slip if she wants to, Emma. Who's the bride here, after all?"

That was the end of the discussion, for Lily was; Lily was the bride.

Mrs. Williams finally had the dress undone. The back of it yawned. "Step in or over the head?" she asked.

"Step," Lily said. That way it would never have to touch her face.

They stretched it wide, her mother on one side and Mrs. Williams on the other, and Lily positioned herself in its circle. They pulled it up over her. It wafted air ahead of it, and there was that slight smell again, beneath the potpourri odor it had picked up in Mrs. Bolland's shop—What was that smell? Where had Lily smelled it before?—there and then gone. Lily extended her arms to allow them to be encased. The mothers drew the collar around her neck and set about the tedious work of buttoning the minuscule bridal buttons. "My fingers are so stiff!" and "Mine too!" they chimed. When they had finished at last, they tugged Lily to the mirror and exclaimed over her some, and touched her hips, her shoulders—though Lily noticed that each time they pulled away, quick as instinct, from the feel of the fabric. Then her mother cupped Lily's cheek, and Mrs. Williams stood on a chair to drive the comb of the veil into the back of Lily's head, teeth digging, and the mothers' eyes moistened and leaked (a thing Lily would have thought impossible of the monolithic Mrs. Williams) as they hugged her and cooed and hugged each other. "Your father will come back to get you when it's time," her mother told her, with a little whimper, and handed Lily her bouquet of white roses. Then the mothers were gone, off to take their seats.

Lily, alone. She looked down at the flowers and fingered their springy, resilient petals, considering.

She wasn't really unhappy. She had always looked forward to her wedding. And it wasn't as if she had qualms about Martin himself, who had always been so sweet to her. At the beginning, her friends had all told her to be careful with an older boy, but there had been worship in Martin's eyes and in his fingers when he touched her, so lightly it seemed he considered her some perfectly ripe, bruisable fruit. He held her that way even when they danced. She remembered spinning around her streamered high-school gymnasium with him— and despite the whirling there was still, somehow, almost no force in his hand on her back, in his other hand pressing hers. She'd breathed in—the gym, no matter how transformed, still smelled like a gym—and looked up to find him smiling.

"What?" she said.

"Nothing. I just feel lucky when I look at you."

Between that and the heart's-blood-red of the streamers, reflecting on his face, and the music, Lily had felt like she was in a film.

Martin wrote to her all through his two years away. *When I close my eyes, I can almost see your face.*

She'd written back, *Thinking of you always, my dearest.* Every letter she sent was full of romantic phrasing and pet names: *prince, sweet, darling.* She did not use that kind of language naturally in speech, but she enjoyed the powerful feel of loading her letters with more freight than she thought Martin could easily bear. She'd imagined him reading them in his uniform and shaking for love of her.

Now he was home again, and wasn't that what she had spent all that time wanting? True, he seemed somehow changed, his eyes, fingers, words not quite the same. Last week he'd told her, "Soon you'll be mine," so little mist in his voice she'd been startled. Yet all that was to be expected. Lily's mother said that she must expect changes and that she must be patient, since Martin would of course take some time to get back to himself again.

Lily began to pace back and forth, but the movement of the dress stirred the air and raised the unplaceable hint of the smell again. And there was the sound of the fabric trailing across the carpet behind her, a sound like something creeping stealthily through leaves. So she stood still instead and gazed at herself in the mirror. She turned half to the side and clasped her bouquet low in front of her, which was the pose her mother had struck in her own wedding photograph two decades before. The sight of herself that way made Lily feel better, as if she were inhabiting an already established scene. She took a deep breath that smelled only of the white roses she held, romantic and ceremonial. This is my wedding day, Lily told herself, again.

Soon her father knocked at the door and opened it. "Oh, honey-pie," he said when he saw her, and this made Lily feel better too, and it wasn't hard to smile at him and say "Daddy" and go and kiss him on his fresh-shaved cheek.

She took his arm. He led her in a satisfyingly stately way from the room and toward the sanctuary.

They paused at the start of the aisle. The organ was already playing and the people turned in their seats to look at her. There was Martin, at the front of the church. His uniform made him striking and serious, just the way Lily had hoped. The music shifted to the wedding march, and her Aunt

Nancy appeared out of nowhere to arrange her train, and the people stood up from their seats for Lily, and she was feeling much better, better about everything, until Aunt Nancy fluffed the dress and the breath of it washed over Lily's face just as she was inhaling deeply to steady herself. She had never before gotten so much of the smell into her mouth and nose.

She placed it all at once and irrevocably. The moist smoky smell of meat in a fire.

Where could Martin's parachute have picked up such a smell? Lily wondered, and instantly an answering image rose in her mind. She saw Martin dangling from his parachute, falling through a clear blue foreign sky, closer and closer to men on the ground who were burning, and the screams and the smells they gave off rose, rose, until the parachute caught them and soaked them greedily into its skin, the skin that was now layered over Lily's own. Her father started them down the aisle and Lily went with him blindly. The parachute rustled around her as she moved. The sound somehow shifted the image so that she was no longer watching as Martin dropped from the sky. Instead, she herself was the one descending, tied more tightly to the parachute than Martin had ever been. She saw this and she saw the church before her, Martin and Reverend Barris waiting for her at the front; but she saw them as if they were at the bottom of a long well shaft, down which she was, by slow increments, falling.

THERE IS NO WAY to unsmell a thing once you have smelled it. Lily was able to stand and say her vows and kiss her husband, walk with him back down the aisle. She was able to pose for the camera and then climb with some grace into the car that was waiting to drive them to the reception at the VFW hall, to interlock her fingers with Martin's, to climb out and smile and wave bridally to the people who'd arrived first, to take her place with Martin at the table where their parents were waiting. But through it all the odor lingered in her nostrils in a terrible parody of the campfires of her childhood. She chewed limp salad leaves during dinner and pushed her chicken to one side, hating its weight against the tines of her fork as it slid.

After dessert, Martin reached for Lily's hand and pulled her up. "Come here a minute. I have something to show you."

"They'll miss us," Lily said.

He looked pointedly at their parents. Hers had their eyes on their dinner plates; his were talking to the couple beside them. In fact, though the room was full of people who had come there to see her and Martin, somehow no one was looking at them right at that moment.

Outside the main hall, Martin opened a door on a stairwell and began to climb. He moved quickly, ahead of Lily, as her shoes pinched her toes and the dress snagged on the steps' rough edges. "Slow down!" she said.

"I'm excited for you to see."

At the top of the stairwell he opened another door and led her out into the dark. They were on the roof. Lily had been expecting a room, and the expanse of the sky surprised her. The lights of their town stretched a long way. The night air had a wonderful coolness after the strange warmth of the day; something in Lily's stomach settled for the first time in hours. Martin was watching her face. "Well?" he said.

"I didn't know you could get up here. It's pretty," she said.

Martin drew her to him. He pressed his lips to her forehead, right at the edge of her hairline. He did not seem to smell anything unusual on her. "Not as pretty as you," he said.

That was nice. That was the sort of thing Lily had always thought Martin would tell her on their wedding day. She closed her eyes.

"My Lily-lil. My wifey-wife," he said, and laughed. That was less nice. She could not recall Martin ever before calling her Lily-lil, and there was that painful note to his laughter since he had returned, that scraping of raw parts together. She took a step back, but he grabbed her hand again. "This way."

She followed. He had her hand, after all. "What?"

"You have to come closer to really see."

They stopped just before the railing and stood together. He was right; you did see it differently from here. A carpet of lights was spread below. It was easy to believe that if you stepped out you could drift down and walk across them, that they would warm the soles of your feet. Sounds from the party slipped through the open windows downstairs: the clink of silverware on dishes, someone laughing. Lily straightened her shoulders and tried to breathe the sounds and the lights in.

A movement, a stirring by her legs caught her; Martin had let go of her hand and was fingering the skirt of the dress. He pinched a layer of it between his fingers and lifted it closer to his face. The way he looked at it made Lily feel as if he had forgotten she was there.

"Stop that," she said, harshly. She pushed his hand away. The fabric dropped.

"It's amazing," Martin said. "In the air. Your chute, it sort of slows time down. You're supposed to be falling—all around you things are falling—but you just float."

Lily wasn't sure what she was supposed to say.

"And now, wifey, look at you. You're the one wearing the chute, aren't you?"

A thrill of fear quieted her. It seemed very important to be silent, not to move.

Martin turned to look at her with an evaluating kind of shine in his eye. On his face a smile was growing, growing, a smile that was somehow like the smell she had been smelling all night.

"What do you think, wife? Do you think you would float?"

A rush in her ears, like a current of air. She could not take her eyes from Martin's face, which seemed a sudden horror to her. My God, Lily thought, this is his skin I'm wearing, and now I'm looking at the rest of him—what used to be hidden.

She could try for the stairs. If she darted, she might make it. Down in the main hall she could find someone—her father, her mother—and explain, and surely they would save her. *We see. Of course you don't have to. Of course it doesn't count.*

But they'd made her wear this dress, hadn't they?

So she would pass through the hall and just keep running. Find a car or a bus to get on. People found buses, took them to places. There must after all be other places. The lives Lily could have in those places extended in a hazy multicolored wash, just beyond the rim of the town's lights, vague at such a distance. But in none of them would she have to carry this moment with her forever, listening to it breathe. Imagining every time she looked at Martin—at the dinner table, as they drove down the street, when their eyes met over the head of their first child—how it would feel if he chose that moment to slide the ground out from under her. The drop in her stomach, the feel of every last thing rushing up.

Downstairs, someone shrieked playfully—the sound you make if a handsome boy, one you could possibly love, swipes the napkin from your lap. Floating, Lily thought, was only another word for falling. If Martin took a step toward her, she would scream, and then she would run, and she would figure out where she was going as she went.

He'd heard the noise, too, though. It seemed to loosen something in him.

"Sounds like we're missing quite the time down there," he said. With his head turned that way, she couldn't see his face at all. From this angle he might have been almost anyone. He might have been someone glimpsed once in a crowd, never to be seen again.

IN THE DINING ROOM, Emma noticed a single bridal button on the tablecloth by her daughter's empty seat, looking as unalterably detached as a lost tooth. She plucked it up in a hurry, but the movement drew Sarah's eyes.

"She must have knocked into something," Sarah said. "Loosened the threads."

"Or maybe the material doesn't bear up," Emma said defensively. But it was hard to defend Lily in good faith against charges of carelessness, and she was relieved when Sarah went back to staring in disapproval at the girl two tables over who had shrieked a minute before.

Emma looked down at the button in her palm, wrapped so prettily in silk and edged with tatting. Then she looked around the room at this gathering she had so carefully planned, the tablecloths and shining glassware, all her friends and relations in their best clothes. These, she thought, are the ways we cover over the things that are meant to catch and hold. She could remember very little from her own wedding. So many years ago. Just a happy blur, and music, and her shoes rubbing and giving her blisters, and Gary's face, nervous and lean, so little like his face now.

Gary returned from the drink table, then, and extended his hand to her for a dance. Emma felt very tired, but what could she do? She laid her hand in his.

THE CHURCH LADIES WATCHED the Bakers dance. Some of them were dancing too, with their husbands, or with their husbands' close friends; some of them had worn out their feet, or had more to drink than they'd meant to, and were sitting down. The Bakers shuffled, the Bakers leaned. They reminded the ladies of their own age. Who wanted to watch the Bakers? The ladies wanted to watch the bridal couple, who, yes, would remind them they were old, but also that they used to be young. Where had those brand-new Williamses gone?

Again, the ladies scanned the room, to no avail, and puffed out their faded, powdery cheeks. The ladies were owed this, the sight of the bride and groom, the dress and the uniform, whirling around the room, stitching the past to what came next. Somebody ought to find them and tell them so.

THE RENAISSANCE PERSON TOURNAMENT

THE TOURNAMENT is the highlight of our year at the Simmler School, figuratively and literally: Abe Larson, math teacher and advisor to the tech club, uses acid-bright bulbs in the auditorium spotlights. He likes to make the contestants sweat. Abe is grizzled, ponytailed, a bitter man. The rest of us are bitter too, in our different ways, but most of us try to be less blatant.

I am fluttering-nervous as I wait for the Tournament to begin, though I know this delicate feeling is much too young for me. I sit by myself in the seventh row. Amanda Stevens from the Foreign Language department waved and mouthed "Over here, Julia" as I was coming in, but I pretended not to see her, since I don't have it in me to hear about her fiancé or their kitchen remodel just now. Already the judges on the panel are arrayed at their table and chatting amongst themselves. The reflection of those overdone spotlights on the three contestants' empty chairs makes them look like they're holding shining pools of water. I wonder which one Emily will choose, whether she'll sit between the two boys or on one of the ends.

"Seat taken, Jules?"

No one but Jim Barnham has ever in my life called me Jules. When I turn, he's already sitting. "You nervous?" he says. He leans in, blue eyes beamy. His desperation to be loved is becoming doglike with the years—both of us nearing fifty now.

I will not pet him. I give him a very small smile. "Well, you must be too." Jim and I are the faculty coaches for two of this year's three contestants, the two who have an actual chance of winning: Emily Branch (mine) and Peter Sweeney (his).

"Right, right. The kid is *amazing*, though, which helps. And yours." He does a little whistle and wiggles his eyebrows. I note with satisfaction how they've grown shaggy. The remark and the wiggle feel lifted from the behavior of some effusive jokey man Jim must at some point have studied. I have wondered about the identity of this man from whom Jim borrows, if he is one or a combination of many, real or filmed or written; I've never quite been able to place him. My shame is that at first I failed to see through any of it, just like the generations of students who dedicate the yearbook to Jim with stunning regularity. *Mr. Barnham, YOU CHANGED MY LIFE!!* It took me longer than it should have to understand that there is weakness in a need to make oneself loved, even if one is successful in the attempt.

Despite his contrived mode of expression, Jim isn't wrong about Emily and Peter. They are, both of them, amazing. Emily is just a little bit more amazing.

"We'll see how they do," I say.

They are coming onstage now. All three are laid bare by

those lights. Emily sits, watchful, in the middle. Peter is on her left, looking relaxed except that one foot bounces, and Jeremy Cooper is on her right. Poor Jeremy. He knows what he's in for, blinking out at all of us in his humiliated ferrety way. Jeremy Cooper is here because he is good at memorizing the answers for tests, so he has accumulated, by this point in his junior year, a nice high GPA, and because we needed a third. Even his coach, Ellen Sayers from the Social Studies department, understands that Jeremy has nothing that could let him touch Peter and Emily. I have been grooming Emily for the Tournament since she arrived at Simmler as a ninth grader, and really she's been grooming herself for it all her life. I could tell on the morning I met her. I always open my first lesson of the year with introductions: the students go around the room and say their names, then their favorite books and a couple of words about why they love them. That first morning, Emily said softly, looking at her hands, "*King Lear*. For the *power*." And I was plunged back into my sunny rose-wallpapered high-school bedroom, where I'd read *Lear* for the first time. I remembered the feeling I'd had then, of a voice rising up in me to answer that scale, that heft—a voice larger than mine that still somehow came from me.

I've taught a wealth of bright and talented students. I have watched them in their finest moments and glimpsed the adults they might become, if things go well for them. When I saw the way Samantha Matthews's capable hands calmly patted the back of the crying friend she hugged, I also saw the scrubs her older self could wear. I heard long slick tables and crisp suits in the smooth answers Patrick Dunning gave every time I called on him, whether or not he actually knew anything about what I'd asked. Emily is the only student I've taught whose future remains opaque to me, because nothing I can fix on seems big enough.

Though that's not quite true, that she's the only one. I've never been able to see Peter Sweeney's future either. With

Emily the blank seems too vast to fill, but Peter's blank I can fill with too many things. He performs each task with so little effort that you think he'll be doing it forever, until he does the next thing.

Emily looks calm as she waits, her dark fringe of bangs sleek above her immobile, solemn face. Peter has begun to smile, just the right amount—*so nice to see all of you!*—for the crowd. Jeremy looks like he might throw up.

"All right, everybody!" says Linda Hayes, the head of this year's judging panel. "All right, time to begin. Welcome to this year's Renaissance Person Tournament, and congratulations to our three contestants: Emily Branch, Jeremy Cooper, Peter Sweeney. To have been selected to compete is a very great honor."

We all clap. Jim's elbow brushes mine.

"Round One of the Tournament will consist of three free-response questions that assess the candidates' knowledge of history, culture, and literature. Each candidate, in alphabetical order, will have the opportunity to be first respondent on one question. Miss Emily Branch will begin. She'll have five minutes in which to answer, and then each of the other contestants will have two minutes to respond and add to Miss Branch's response."

Round One is, I think, the easiest—a simple matter of knowing things—but I find I'm gripping my own kneecaps.

"Are you ready, Miss Branch?"

"Yes."

"Here is your question. Please discuss the agenda of the First Council of Nicaea, the degree to which that agenda was successfully completed, and the long-term effects of the Council on history and culture. You have five minutes. Your time begins now."

Emily bows her shining head, also wetted by the lights. I try to keep breathing. Why doesn't she start?

At last she raises her face. "We believe," she says, "in one God, the Father Almighty, Maker of all things visible and invisible, And in one Lord..."

Reciting the entire thing this way will eat up her time, but Emily has chosen to do it for the sake of performance. She is giving us the original Nicene Creed from the First Council. I hadn't even known she knew it. Her voice is unhurried, not overly loud, and the words click out smooth as pearls she is dropping onto a string. I listen as she comes to the end. She'll have only a couple of minutes left to say anything of her own. "...they are condemned by the holy and apostolic Catholic church."

Emily pauses for the space of a breath.

"I think this speech, the first version of the Nicene Creed, is the most important development to emerge from the First Council of Nicaea of 325 C.E. The Council had many purposes. To settle the Arian and Meletian controversies. To fix on a definitive Easter date. To decide questions about baptism and the persecution of nonbelievers. Each of these was resolved, and all of that is important. But I'm not sure anything is more important than the *words*. With the Creed, the Council members were declaring that they had the right to control and unify the beliefs of the faithful. They took many voices and"—another pause—"*braided* them into one. With this Creed, the Council reaches through time to shape even my voice, even today. It's amazing, I think, that words can do that. They can *change* you, if you let them." A shyness comes into her voice, because she's describing the shape of her own life so far. The corners of her mouth lift slightly. "If you want them to."

Emily stops, just as Linda's teeth are coming together to tell her *time*. There's a short silence. I wish I could record its awed sound.

"Thank you, Miss Branch," Linda says. To her credit, her

voice is almost neutral. "Mr. Cooper, you will respond first. Your two minutes begin now."

Jeremy's ears and nose begin to go red. "Well," he says. Maybe feeling the way his nose is turning on him, he rubs at it. "I think Emily covered things pretty well. I guess I'd just add that the Council happened in 325 C.E."

Emily said that. The judges' pencils move discreetly.

"And that the Arian controversy had to do with—" He panics as he realizes he can't come up with the word, which is *Trinitarianism.* I watch Emily ache to whisper it to him. "With whether Jesus was, in actuality, divine. Where his place was, relative to God." It feels as if the judges' busy pencils are scratching at Jeremy's skin. "That's it, really," Jeremy says. Ellen said he was excited when she told him he was the faculty's choice to be the third competitor. I know she did her best to help him prepare, and I know he'd have been diligent in reading whatever she gave him. But he's a kid who's spent years reading only the texts his teachers have given him, though very thoroughly, and that's not the kind of study the Tournament rewards; what's fair game is too wide-ranging.

"You still have about a minute, if you want to use it," Linda tells him gently. Jeremy shakes his head.

"Okay, then. Mr. Sweeney, your turn. Two minutes."

"Thank you," Peter Sweeney says. He smiles again for all of us. He has an almost perfect face, lean and warm, classic as something from a dated book in which the hero is described as *dashing.* "My fellow contestants have made excellent points. I liked Jeremy's emphasis on Arianism, on the Trinitarian controversy." Flawlessly done: he's pointed out Jeremy's mistake while underscoring his own command, yet he manages to disguise the jab as graciousness. "And Emily, Emily makes such an eloquent, powerful point, about voices."

This is when Emily blushes. I have never in all the time that I have known her seen Emily Branch blush. As her cheeks stain pink, I feel a dark dread well in the back of my throat.

"Of course, neither of those are really *lasting* develop-
ments. Constantine, who called the Council, was succeeded
by two emperors who restored Arianism for a time. And the
First Nicene Creed was later revised into the Second Nicene
Creed, the version so many of us are familiar with today: 'We
believe in one God, the Father Almighty, *Maker of Heaven and
Earth,*' and so on."

I am sure to the bottom of my soul that Peter knows no
more than this of the Nicene Creed in either version. This is
his genius, to make the things he doesn't know look unwor-
thy of attention: *and so on.*

"So for *me* the lasting effect of the Nicene Council is something else. It has to do with the fact that all of these bishops
arrive in Nicaea *because Constantine has called them.* With the
fact that great events and decisions can be controlled by *one
great man.*"

He finishes just as his two minutes come to a close. *Look at
me,* his face tells us. *I will be a great man. I'm not that far from
being one already.*

I FIND EMILY AFTERWARD. I pull her carefully to me, as if she
were an injured bird, though when I release her, her face is
untroubled. Round One has left her one point behind Peter.
She won the First Responses—Peter's was polished and impressive but nothing like the miracle of hers—and of course she
carried the Second Responses against Jeremy, bringing her to
eight points total. Peter, who won both his rounds of Second
Responses and took second place in the First Responses, has
nine. Jeremy has two points, having placed third in the First
Responses. We give points for third place out of three because
we're teachers, and we like to be encouraging.

"The Nicene Creed," I say to her, shaking my head. "The
first Nicene Creed."

She shrugs. "I'm happy with how it went," she says. A

typical Emily remark—I'm used to congratulating her while she looks at the floor. But today she's watching Peter, across the room, as Jim claps him on the back.

Peter meets her gaze and smiles. That smile is something that should only be turned on many people at once. It's heavy as gold, and I don't think even Emily can be expected to bear up under it.

THE NEXT MORNING I'm in my classroom early, anticipating that Emily will come see me, as she usually does. "It sort of settles me into the day," she told me once.

While I wait, I straighten the chairs around my oval table. I like them even-spaced as good teeth. I've done this each school morning for twenty years, since I first came to Simmler when I was twenty-eight. My classroom by now is my own kingdom. Everything in it I have chosen: the posters of the Globe Theater and wry-eyed Hannah Arendt, the pieces of yellow, not white, chalk that I keep lined up in dusty parade in the tray beneath the board, the bright throw rugs I've scattered around the edges of the room, every book on the three big bookshelves.

If this room is a kingdom, though, its citizens are not only my students, past and present, but also the different people I have been, all these years. The books remind me most of the fall I turned thirty, when I was wondering whether or not to leave Simmler and apply to graduate school—when I would walk away from the grading spread on my desk, lift a book from the shelf, and ruffle its pages, trying to decide if I was brave enough to venture in again, alone, to wander around and ponder, or if it was too late for that. The window reminds me of the spring ten years ago when my mother died, the most beautiful spring I can remember. Every morning brought buttery light caked thick over the discussion table, so that I was unsure whether feeling or just the glare made my eyes well.

And that back corner, against one of the bookshelves, will always be the place where Jim Barnham feathered his fingers over my collarbone, one early winter afternoon in my first year of teaching (I favored scoop-necked blouses in those days, even in cold weather), during one of the visits he used to pay me between classes. I remember he told me I looked Grecian. This has never been remotely true—I come from Pennsylvania farming stock and I have always looked like I should be hauling hay with my four sturdy sons. Though some part of me knew it was a lie even then, I remember craning my thick neck, in response, as if it were sculpture. This was maybe two weeks before he arrived at the annual Christmas party with the girl who would become his first wife, with nary a word to me. He met her when she sold him a set of salt-and-pepper shakers at the gift store downtown for his mother's Christmas present. In my imagination those salt-and-pepper shakers have always been shaped like ducks.

Emily is late. Her father, who is an electrician, times her rides in the mornings around his own first job of the day. I return to my desk to test my pens. I find two likely to call it quits soon and toss them before they can turn on me.

"Ms. Alberts?" Peter Sweeney is leaning aesthetically against my door frame. "Could I come in for a second? If you're not too busy."

"Sure, Peter. Have a seat."

Even his movements are compliments: he pats the surface of my desk in appreciation, he settles with visible comfort into the chair where Emily should be sitting. "Thanks," he says. "I thought—I hope I'm not interrupting. It's just, you know, they tell us we should ask for lots of people's advice about the Tournament. So I thought I'd stop by, since there's really no one else whose advice I'd rather have. Aside from Mr. Barnham, of course."

Exactly the speech I would expect Peter Sweeney to make

when approaching his opponent's coach. I've never been as fond of Peter as everyone else is. This despite his obvious brilliance—he wrote a paper in my ninth-grade class that I'm not sure I could have written myself—and his generosity to every person around him, even, or especially, the bumblers, the awkward blurters, the strangely dressed, the pockmarked. Other teachers wax rhapsodic about Peter in faculty meetings. Me, I feel certain he wouldn't be so kind if there weren't other people watching. There's a memory I return to when people praise him, a moment that happened when Peter was in ninth grade. He was leaving my room after class with shaggy Sam Evans, who gave up on Simmler midway through that year. Sam had lost his copy of *Romeo and Juliet* again. As they made their way to the door Peter said Sam could borrow his—just come by his locker, Peter told him, with that ease he was already perfecting, as they passed my desk. Right after they'd gone I remembered someone I needed to catch between classes and ducked into the hall.

"So I'll just come up with you?" I heard Sam saying. "Thanks a lot."

And I watched Peter say nothing, turn his perfect back and walk away.

"Peter!" I called. I came up behind them. "Peter, Sam's asking if he can come get your book."

"Oh, sorry," Peter said. "Didn't hear." But in the first moment he turned toward us, just before he composed his face, I saw anger. Gone almost too quickly to register. Still, I saw it, and I know what it was—though he was smart enough to be careful, even then, and I never saw another moment like that from him. He would never make that kind of mistake now.

I fold my hands on my desktop. "I doubt you need much advice, Peter. But of course if I can help I'm happy to."

"What I wanted to ask is—do you have any tips for dealing with the nerves?"

I stare at him. I almost laugh.

"It'll be harder today than yesterday. Because today's about our own opinion, you know? And with all those people watching." He looks at me earnestly. I wonder if he's practiced that look in the big, heavy-framed mirror I'm sure hangs somewhere in his house, maybe above the living-room mantel. "I just figured you might have some thoughts to share, out of your own experience."

All right, I decide. *All right, Peter, let's play.* I knit my eyebrows as if considering what wisdom to bestow. "Well," I tell him, "I think the *best* thing is just to give the most honest, thoughtful answer you can."

"Right," he says. "Thanks. That helps a lot."

"And really, you can't worry about what anyone else's answer will be like. If one of them knows a little more than you, has a little more to say, I mean—" I smile kindly. "You don't have any control over that, do you? All you can do is your own best."

I don't know quite what I'm expecting, but I know that it isn't for Peter to return my smile, sunnily, as he does. "You're talking about Emily, I guess," he says. "You must be so proud of her. She's really—incredible."

That breaks me out of our nice game. *You stay away from her*, I think.

He's standing up now. "Well, I should be going," he says. "I'm sure she'll be wanting to talk to you too."

I collect myself enough to say, "Good luck today, Peter," emphasizing *luck* just a little, but he's already out the door, and I don't know if he hears.

In the quiet of my kingdom then, I continue to wait for Emily. Five minutes before the start of first period I go upstairs and find her with some other junior girls, all of them leaning against the lockers with their legs stretched out into the hall. "Oh, hi," Emily tells me.

I have given this girl stacks of books, careful criticism and more careful encouragement, raw and beating belief. Hours and hours and hours of my life, so that she might have the chance to stand up and prove what she can do, so that she will be able to carry the record of that proof inside herself, reinforcing that self's outline, forever. The Tournament itself is a small thing, but what it could do for Emily is not small. There aren't that many chances like this in a life, though she can't yet see that. I force myself to speak calmly. "I thought maybe you'd want to come down and talk."

"I was just feeling pretty ready," she tells me. "I wasn't sure I needed to."

What she's doing instead, I suspect, is sitting here for the chance that Peter Sweeney might walk by.

CLASSES ARE ALL FIVE MINUTES shorter than usual to make time for Round Two of the Tournament at the end of the day. The difference is slight but noticeable to all of us; when your time and thought are habitually carved up into forty-minute increments, each thirty-five minute class has the short, wincing feel of a limp. Before I know it I'm back in the auditorium.

I see Jim three rows back, chatting with Amanda Stevens, who has her head back, laughing, in the posture of the deliciously teased. Her throat is pink. I wonder what her fiancé would have to say about this particular picture, if he could see it.

I slide into the chair on the other side of Jim, and he turns toward me, his face folding over on itself with happiness. Being chosen, by anyone, is one of Jim's favorite things.

"Hey, Emily did great yesterday," he says, with a magnanimous sweep of his hands.

"Thanks."

Amanda feels the warm tide of his attention turn from her and swivels to talk to Stan Fisher, who teaches French. Some sleeping muscle deep within me takes this for a triumph, and twitches with a remembered, irrelevant pleasure. That twitch, it makes me angrier.

"Jim, can I ask you something?"

"Ask away."

"Have you gotten the feeling that Peter is *interested*, you know, in Emily?"

"I've been thinking that too."

I nod, pressing my teeth together very hard. Because I know Peter isn't interested in Emily, not really—only in making her think he is. When has Peter ever felt a true thing? Except perhaps his desire to win.

"I think he admires her," Jim tells me. "And I think that's beginning to grow into something more." His tone is as jolly as if we're discussing the mating of prize pets. The thing is, I'm not even sure it's an act, his taking Peter's interest at face value. I doubt he bothers to think much about what goes on inside Peter's head.

"Very natural," Jim says.

Blessedly I don't have to comment on the naturalness of it all, because Alex Wells is bringing Jeremy out of the holding tank and onto the stage. The order has been chosen from a hat: Jeremy, then Peter, then Emily. Each contestant will deliver a speech, composed on the spot, on the same topic, while the other two wait in the hall with a teacher so there's no chance for them to overhear. Today Jeremy has the look of someone being led to his place of execution. He stands, center stage, and waits for the blow.

"Here is your assigned topic, Mr. Cooper. Please give us your opinion on the following: what is the single most important moral value a perfect society should hold? You have five minutes, beginning now."

About as generic and open-ended a question as possible; the idea in Round Two is to leave them plenty of rope to hang themselves. Which is just what Jeremy proceeds to do—though to be fair to him, maybe it only seems that way in comparison to the performance I know the other two will give. Shiny with sweat, Jeremy starts to talk about *freedom* and then changes direction and focuses on *achievement* instead. The moon landing, the theory of relativity, a vague reference to "literature." It seems that according to Jeremy's definition, we're all living in the perfect society. By the end of the second minute he's back to *freedom* again. He starts talking about the American Revolution, with the upturn at the end of each sentence that I remember from all of his comments in my class, even the smartest ones, and soon he's just reciting the names and dates of acts and battles. This is the kind of mind he has. As we all knew.

Meanwhile, Emily and Peter sit in the hallway. Their supervisor is Mary Alice Washburn, who never seems able to make eye contact with anyone for too long—one of the reasons she's a bad teacher. I wonder just how fast and far Peter's hands might creep in the intervals when Mary Alice is staring at the wall or the floor.

"All of that was because of freedom," Jeremy says. "Freedom is—people are willing to *die* for freedom."

The panel waits for a moment to be sure he's done. Then Linda tells him "Thank you" in a very kind voice. Alex goes back to fetch Peter.

If Jeremy looked like he was being brought to his death, Peter looks like he's going to an awards ceremony to claim his prize. He walks with easy-to-afford modesty, the suggestion that it would be bad taste to draw attention to his victory, that obvious thing. He grins and tents his pockets with his hands while he waits for Linda to tell him the topic. Then he considers.

"The first thing to decide, of course, is the definition of a perfect society," he says, and he's off and running, talking about individuals and community. The rhythm of it is nice. But as I listen, I begin to feel a mounting excitement. "A perfect society," Peter says, "must be deemed perfect by its inhabitants. Each and every one of them must be free to find their own perfection, their own greatness."

All quite unobjectionable on its own, but surely that word *greatness* is tripping the same wire for the judges that it is for me; surely they too are remembering that it's what Peter emphasized in Round One as well. We're hearing ego in a way we would never in a million years hear it from Emily, who has an air of continuous, delighted surprise to have found herself with all of us, away from the small disheveled house that holds the rest of her life.

I'm drifting along on the current of my happiness when I hear something that snags me. "The greatness of a perfect society's individual members should be knit into the general tapestry," Peter says. "Because society is a wonderful contradiction—many and one at once."

The words blend with the rest, but that description of society's nature is Emily's. It's something that I have heard her say, more than once, word for word.

I can see what must have happened. They were preparing for this round together, maybe right out there in the hall, talking over potential questions and ideas that might be dropped into a response. But hearing him say it, I feel as if Peter has reached down Emily's throat, into the core of her, and stolen her words.

This feeling grows when it's Emily's turn, for the line is one of the first things she says. "Society in general strikes me as a beautiful contradiction. It's many and it's one—it's both." Anybody could reason through, could understand that it could be either one's idea. The ear, though, can't forget who said it first. And Peter would have known that very well, as he opened his mouth to say it.

In the wake of that doubling, it's hard, probably, for everyone but me to really listen to the rest of what Emily has to say. "We're all privileged to be a part of such a mechanism—or such an *organism*, really, because society I think is a living body. The work of making it as perfect as it can be, that's a responsibility that ultimately rests with each of us."

Peter comes out ahead in this round by two more points. Linda announces the scores with the three contestants lined up beside her on the stage. As they turn to go, I see Peter's fingertips alight on Emily's shoulder blade. She looks at him, at this thief, with gratitude.

AT TWENTY OF EIGHT on the final morning of the Tournament, I go upstairs to the lockers, because this time I know better than to wait for Emily to come to me. I intercept her at the back of a clump of giggling girls on the move. Though he's nowhere I can see, Peter is all over her: in the toe of her shoe dragging at the floor, in her fingers tucking at her hair. He has pulled her right into the pit of normal vapid adolescence and made her indistinguishable from the indistinguishable girls around her. I know, I do know, that she is just a girl, as they are girls, and so she has every right to feel the same things they do. But it hurts me that it would be hard to pick Emily out now as the one who will go into the auditorium this afternoon and recite an original composition, then gracefully critique the work of her fellow contestants, as Round Three requires. Emily's is an actual, real villanelle, because she loves Bishop's "One Art." Hers isn't a perfect poem—she's only sixteen—but it contains a depth of feeling that astonishes me. I stare at this girl in front of me without recognition. The bored set of the mouth.

"Emily, can I talk to you for a second?" I ask.

"I was just on my way to the bathroom."

She owes this to both of us, though, even if she's lost sight of that now. I raise my eyebrows and say, "I'll see you in my classroom right afterward."

When she arrives, I wait for her to sit, which she does without looking at me. Then I tell her, "I'm worried, Emily."

A standard teacher line, but Emily has probably never before heard it. Her head snaps up. "You aren't happy with how I'm doing?"

"I'm not worried about the *scores.*" I wonder how to explain it to her: that it's the way she's playing that frightens me. That in her life she has the capacity to become wondrous, but not if she makes the choice I fear she's making while we all watch, to put something else ahead of her brain. It's not a choice you get to revise later. You think it is, while you're succumbing to an experience of love that really you're lifting right out of all of your books—while your skin hums and the air grows gold tinted, while his gaze makes you feel you're blooming. The books themselves make you think that maybe books aren't the most important thing after all, or at least that there will be plenty of time to return to them. And I suppose there might be. Time isn't really the problem. It's that when you go to look for those books—if you do go to look—they aren't where you left them, aren't in any place you know, anymore, how to find.

"I just feel like you're losing your focus," I tell Emily.

She hunches her shoulders. In that motion I see a thousand defiant kids who have shrugged, over the years, to tell me they can't do any better, and what do I want from them, exactly? What I want from, for, Emily is the whole world. I want her to feed herself, to watch that self become the most enormous thing.

I wait for her to speak. She won't be able to pretend to be this other girl while she's talking. But she's quiet.

"Emily, listen. Peter, he's—not a good use of your time," I tell her.

That startles her. She didn't think I knew, maybe. "Why?"

Because, I want to tell her, you are so much more

extraordinary than he is. He is only very charming, and too clever to be caught being anything he doesn't want to be. These are not talents; they're weapons. Even when he breaks your heart—and he will, Emily—he'll do it in such a way, I know it, that you won't be able to hate him. You will be left with no one to hate but yourself.

Emily sits as still, now, as a painted girl, waiting for my response. My heart beats furiously with the need to show her the truth. This is Peter, and if I want proof of what I know, I will have to make it.

"This is hard to say," I tell her. "I saw him. With Jessica Fuller, Emily. I'm sorry."

"What do you mean?"

I crease my face in sympathy.

"No," she says, shaking her head. "He hates Jessica."

"Is that what he told you?"

I've chosen well. Jessica has a loud laugh, a habit of wearing skirts so short and tight they're like rubber bands around her hard little backside. I watch Emily begin to doubt. "You must have seen something that *looked* like—"

"Emily, he was kissing her. Up against the lockers."

"When?" she asks, and I know I've done it.

"Yesterday."

She nods rapidly, dry-eyed. Only the ferocity of the motion of her head gives her away. No one has to put that much force into accepting something unless it feels like the end of the world. Who am I to be ending Emily's world, Emily whom I love? But before I can say anything else, she's getting up. "Thanks, Ms. Alberts," she says, her back already to me, and then she's gone.

FOR THE REST OF THE SCHOOL DAY the discussions I am meant to be leading flow past without touching me. We are talking about *The Odyssey*, stranded in one of those endless books after Odysseus has made it home but before he does any suitor-slaughtering. "Why do you think Athena is so *frustrated* with Odysseus here?" I ask. Thirteen faces turn toward me, so pure and blank the sight of them hurts. I want to tell them all to run.

At last Round Three's beginning nears. In the faculty room, I refill my all-day mug and stand by the sink, my back to the other buzzing teachers, to sip the burnt-out end-of-afternoon coffee. There in the basin sits a collection of the many things we leave behind when we flee this room, realizing we have only a minute left before the next class starts: plates smeared with food; cups, their rims bedecked with the half-moons of our bad lipstick shades; sticky and bent-tined forks. These items move from shelf to table to sink in a constant orbit day after day, year after year, as our faces line and the skin of our hands goes baggy. I left a plate in here this morning, I know, but I can't identify it in the heap now.

The room has begun to empty. I've been waiting for this moment for the three years I've known Emily, but I'm not sure I can go down there.

When Jim pops in to check his mailbox, I'm the only other person left in the room. He catches sight of me and grins. "One to go!" he says. He steps over to the photocopier to run something off, a handout for tomorrow, probably, then turns back to me. "I tell you, I can't wait till it's over. The stress!" He ruffles at the back of his hair.

He adopted this mode with me almost right away after that Christmas party twenty years ago: the pretense that we have always been friendly acquaintances. I've come to feel almost grateful for the easy erasure. But I think Jim would be surprised how I still remember. I went alone to the party. I'd assumed Jim would pick me up and we'd go together, but he'd been vague about plans earlier in the week, and when I called him that afternoon he wasn't home, or wasn't answering. So I drove myself to Stacy Porter's house. I wore a wool skirt and a peach-colored cashmere sweater I loved the feel of. I thought his hands would soon be on it, maybe when we stepped outside during the party to stand in the cold: there would be clouds of our breath and the weight of his palms on my shoulders, and the joy of being soft. Jim wasn't there yet when I got to Stacy's, so I spent an hour moving from circle to circle of teachers and laughing politely at displays of intelligence disguised as jokes. Teachers are used to having captive audiences, and it makes us bad at conversation. I held my drink at a pretty angle; I thought, then, that there was a pretty angle for holding a drink. I felt in those days of Jim as if everything I did were suddenly visible.

I saw him right away when he arrived. The door opened and he sidled through, eyes already crinkled, beginning to shrug off his coat. I started to go to him. Then a woman stepped into the entryway. She wore a short sparkly gold dress like she thought this was a nightclub, makeup I could see across the room. I was thinking that Jim and I could laugh about her together, speculate about who she was and invent scandalous explanations for her presence here, when I saw him put his hand, with unmistakable intimacy, to the small of her back.

Now, I know many things about Jim Barnham. I know that beneath his charisma is nothing very genuine or remarkable, really. I know how he married the gold-dressed woman, Ally, and how their marriage lasted the six years until she found out about Laura, who would become his second wife, to whom he would manage to stay married for almost ten. I know he couldn't have given me anything lasting. At some point, even if Ally had not been working that shift at the gift shop, I would have regretted all of it. The regret might as well have arrived when it did.

Yet the suspicion comes to me now that I made some mistake in that moment when I saw him across Stacy Porter's faux-French living room—red cheeked from the cold and from whatever he'd been drinking with Ally—and didn't go to him. I ran instead out the back door and around to my car, then drove home with the radio on to drown out the low, ugly sounds of my own crying, wiping my eyes and nose on the back of my hand. I woke late the next morning and graded papers without leaving the house all day, some of the lowest grades I ever gave.

I wonder if, in that moment when I let Jim have that night just as he wanted it, without even making him explain, I lost something more important than Jim himself. If he was only the shape I gave my loss, because it seemed to want a face. If it was then, exactly then, that I allowed my life to become smaller.

Jim wrinkles his eyebrows at me. "You all right, Jules?"

He asks so lightly, because he doesn't have to care about the answer. I don't want to just release him again, untouched. I cross the room. He moves over, as if he's expecting me to go to my mailbox, but I move over with him. He comes up against the humming, rattling photocopier.

"Jules," he says, his voice warmer than his wary face—a tone you might use to wake up an old friend who'd dozed off on your couch. I bring my face in close to his. I know what I look like at so small a remove: there are folds in my neck and a heaviness to my skin, a wateriness to my eyes. Jim looks older too, since the last time we were this close. But really I'm not seeing Jim at all. I'm seeing a dividing line between possibilities and impossibilities, glowing like a live wire there in front of me. If I brought my lips to his I might still catch its taste: the electric spark of an open world.

Down below us, on the first floor, Emily walks toward the auditorium. Inside, she will recite her villanelle with her dark, magical eyes on the ceiling. "The house is mine, and I know all its lines. / I could draw them: roof and floor, each wall. / Its rooms are holes I feel along my spine..."

The lights will heat Emily's skin like tiny, loving suns. If she gives her whole self, as she will do, in exchange we will heat her to the point where no one can touch her, and then release her to scorch a path through the rest of her life. I don't even ask to watch that next part. I don't particularly expect her to remember me then. Only this part, only the readying and the imagining of what may come next, belongs to me.

Emily will feel hot, on that stage. As she describes her house, she will see it. She will feel the way she has felt, living inside it. Inside herself. I have thought about those feelings until I've been sure I've understood them, but after all I have only been seeing them from the outside.

Jim's eyes are desperately seeking a safe space somewhere off to the side of me. I lean closer still, so he has no choice but to look where I want him to. See? There I am. Still there.

"We should go down," Jim says. He sounds almost afraid. "They'll be looking for us."

Our students, he means. Will they? I'm not sure. Peter looks only for what he needs.

And Emily? Emily may or may not look for me in the crowd, while she speaks. She may or may not look for Peter. We will all be looking at her, watching for her poem to emerge, holding our breath. We want it to be unlike anything we've ever seen, and we also want to recognize it. But when it does emerge, Emily won't wait for us. She will send it walking down the aisle, and I'll be just like all the others, lucky to catch the flash of its face before it's out the door.

ACKNOWLEDGMENTS

FINALLY, I GET TO THANK the people without whom this book would not exist. The editors whose magazines and anthologies first published these stories shaped them, gave them a home, and gave me faith: James Scott, Hannah Tinti, Sam Ligon, Jennifer Acker, Anna Lena Phillips Bell, Beth Staples, Arijit Sen, Brian Lee, Dave Eggers, Jesse Nathan, Carmen Johnson, Caitlin Horrocks, David Lynn, Abigail Serfass, and Halimah Marcus.

To everyone at Lookout Books: I won when you took me on. Emily Smith, what you've done for this book is sorcery. Beth Staples, my dream editor, possessed of magical eye and heart and mind: you know and understand these stories as well as I do, and have made them, in every case, into truer, more powerful versions of themselves. I could not be more grateful.

Michelle Brower is the smartest, kindest, most patient, most loyal, most indefatigable, and best agent in all the land.

Thank you to the Bread Loaf Writers' Conference, for support and for giving me a writing community at a time when it sometimes felt like most of my life was spent changing diapers. Thank you to the National Endowment for the Arts for the dizzying gift, and the accompanying, invaluable gift of belief.

I'm grateful to all of my teachers, especially Chang-rae Lee, Joyce Carol Oates, Sam Lipsyte, Ursula Hegi, Edmund White, Mark Slouka, Jon Dee, and Binnie Kirshenbaum. And to all of my classmates.

To Megan Mayhew Bergman, for being generous beyond measure, time and time again. To Morgan Davis and Susan White, for thoughtful fact checking. To Erin Kottke, incredible, big-hearted advocate.

My brilliant Tahoe women, Kara Levy, Helene Wecker, Michelle Adelman, Ruth Galm—you and your work inspire me, and your companionship in this arena is worth more to me than I will ever be able to tell you. And Ruth, several of these stories wouldn't be the same without you and your rare vision. Keri Bertino, my talented and wise writing buddy, you keep me afloat. Thank you all.

I'm grateful to my wonderful friends, new and old. Amy Wu Silverman, Anna Mirabile, and Kate Schlesinger have been patiently listening to me fret about writing since college, and Lydia Nycz has been listening for even longer. I'm so lucky to have every one of you; you are my favorites. Boston friends, I miss you daily. Pittsburgh friends, it isn't such an easy thing to move to a brand-new city with a six-month-old, but you have made it home.

I'm grateful to my students, over the years, at St. Vincent College, the Pittsburgh Center for the Arts, and Falmouth Academy. You have all enriched my life. And to the FA teachers who were my colleagues, some of the smartest, best people on the planet, who helped me become a grownup.

And last, to my family. Thank you, all of you. Thank you to my brother, Owen Beams, who's off in the world doing hard, important work, and raising his beautiful family, and making me very proud. To my dad, Mark Beams, who showed me a long time ago what it looked like to live a good life, and has helped me, in every conceivable way, to create my own. To my mom, Ann Beams, who reads more than anyone I know, and whose unconditional belief and love and championing have been some of the greatest gifts of my life.

Tess, you brought all kinds of wonder with you into the world—and continue to. Being your mom is the luckiest thing that has happened to me yet.

And Finnegan Calabro, partner of every dream—you make all things possible.

These stories originally appeared, sometimes in different form, in the following publications: "The Drop" in the *Common,* "The Saltwater Cure" in *Day One,* "Granna" in *Ecotone,* "All the Keys to All the Doors" in Electric Literature's *Recommended Reading,* "We Show What We Have Learned" in *Hayden's Ferry Review* and *The Best American Nonrequired Reading 2011,* "Ailments" in the *Kenyon Review,* "World's End" in *One Story,* and "Hourglass" in *Willow Springs.*

Lookout Books

Lookout is more than a name—it's our
publishing philosophy. Founded as the
literary book imprint of the Department
of Creative Writing at the University of
North Carolina Wilmington, Lookout seeks
out works by emerging and historically
underrepresented voices, as well as
overlooked gems by established writers.
In a publishing landscape increasingly
indifferent to literary innovation, Lookout
offers a haven for books that matter.

TEXT NEW BASKERVILLE ITC PRO   10.7 / 13.5
DISPLAY BEBAS NEUE   16